Math
Mysteries

For Dad, who knows his math

An imprint of Macmillan Children's Publishing Group, LLC
120 Broadway, New York, NY 10271 • OddDot.com • mackids.com
Odd Dot ® is a registered trademark of Macmillan Publishing Group, LLC

WRITER Aaron Starmer
ILLUSTRATOR Marta Kissi
DESIGNER Caitlyn Hunter
EDITOR Justin Krasner

Library of Congress Control Number: 2022920564

Our books are available at special discounts when purchased in bulk for
premiums and sales promotions as well as for fund-raising or educational
use. Special editions or book excerpts also can be created to specification.
For details, contact the Macmillan Corporate and Premium Sales
Department at (800) 221-7945 ext. 5442, or send an email to
MacmillanSpecialMarkets@macmillan.com.

First edition, 2023

Printed in the United States of America by
Lakeside Book Company, Crawfordsville, Indiana

ISBN 978-1-250-83928-2 (paperback)

1 3 5 7 9 10 8 6 4 2

ISBN 978-1-250-88957-7 (hardcover)

1 3 5 7 9 10 8 6 4 2

Joyful Books for Curious Minds

Math Mysteries

THE TRIPLET THREAT

GABE

ABBY

CAM

the PRIME DETECTIVES

By Aaron Starmer

Illustrations by Marta Kissi

Odd Dot New York

Chapter 1

THE CASE OF
THE EXTRA TEN MINUTES

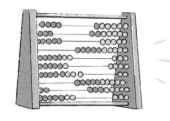

Some people say that three is a magic number, and they might be right. It depends on whether you believe in magic.

Abby "the Abacus" Feldstein believed in magic, or at least she believed in the magic of three. When she was three years old, she had discovered that she could easily add and subtract by the number three in her head. She soon came to believe that other numbers were magical, too. All numbers. But three would always hold a special place in her heart.

Triangles had three sides, and her favorite food, Doritos, were triangles. She had three cats: Boogie, Bumpus, and Doug. And she often tied her hair into three ponytails, with two on the sides and one in the back.

Third grade at Arithmos Elementary School had been a magical year for Abby as well. It was the year when she had memorized pi to the thirty-third decimal place: 3.141592653589793238462643 383279502. She had also learned to solve a Rubik's Cube in thirty-three seconds using the Fridrich method. But most importantly, she had teamed up with two friends: Cameron "Cam" McGill and Gabriel "Gabe" Kim. And together, the three of them became known as the Prime Detectives.

The name had at least two meanings. The first meaning had to do with quality. If there was a mystery to be solved, they were the best kids for the job. Usually, they were the only kids for the job, but that didn't matter. They were always top-tier, grade-A investigators.

The second meaning was related to math. In math, a prime number is a number that cannot be divided by any numbers other than one and itself. One hundred four thousand seven hundred twenty-nine is a prime number. So is three. The three kids always worked together when confronting a problem. Together they were more than the sum of their parts. And they could not be split up. They were indivisible.

In other words, they were prime detectives. In more ways than one.

And how did the Prime Detectives solve mysteries? With numbers, of course!

Whenever there was a problem at school, Abby, Cam, and Gabe were on the case. Using arithmetic, geometry, and logic, the Prime Detectives figured out who did what and when. And often why!

There had been *The Case of the Dribbling Water Fountain*, which they cracked by calculating water pressure and borrowing a pipe wrench. Determining the circumference of a circle and laying out some enticing banana slices helped them solve *The Case of the Escaped Hamster*. And if they didn't know fractions, they never would've figured out *The Case of the Missing Piece of Pizza*. But they did know fractions, so the missing piece of pizza was found. And eaten.

However, that had been third grade. And third grade was over.

The first day of fourth grade at Arithmos Elementary started ominously. That means some weird and spooky things happened.

As Abby, Cam, and Gabe were approaching the school, the custodian, Mrs. Vernon, walked past them on her way to the outdoor toolshed. She was pushing a wheelbarrow, and it had a blanket over the top of it, hiding something. Strange sounds, like chirps and growls and whistles, could be heard from under the blanket, which was intriguing but also a little frightening. So they hurried inside as quickly as possible.

As they were walking down the hall toward their classroom, they noticed a few dark splatter stains on the walls. *Blood?* They hoped not!

Finally, when Abby, Cam, and Gabe entered their classroom, they found that there was a small, black-feathered bird perched on their teacher's desk.

"Is that . . . normal?" Cam asked.

"For an aviary," Gabe said. "Or a haunted mansion."

"Shoo," Abby said, waving her arms at the

bird. It turned its head, gave her a dirty look, then flapped its shimmery wings and flew out of an open window.

"Later, birdbrain," a voice said.

It was their teacher's voice. She was standing in the doorway, wearing a long white dress that was covered in swirling and complicated math equations. It looked as if someone had stolen a whiteboard from NASA and printed it on a piece of fabric. Even Abby, who was a math whiz, didn't understand a single equation on it.

The teacher's name was Mrs. Everly, but everyone called her Mrs. E.

The Prime Detectives knew who she was, but this was their first time officially meeting her.

"Hi, Mrs. E., I'm Cam McGill," Cam said, putting out a hand. "Pleasure to make your acquaintance."

Mrs. E. shook his hand. "A pleasure to make your acquaintance as well, Cam," she said, then she turned to the other two. "And you must be Abby Feldstein and Gabe Kim."

Cam might have been naturally friendly, but Gabe was naturally suspicious. "How did you know that?" he asked.

"Everyone knows about the Prime Detectives," Mrs. E. said. "You saved Thanksgiving last year."

This was only partly true, but Cam was happy to take credit. "We did it all for the mashed potatoes, Mrs. E. No one should ever miss out on mashed potatoes."

"Agreed. And I've heard you're quite the good cook. Is that true, Cam?" Mrs. E. asked as she walked over to her desk, which sat in the corner of the room.

"No one complains when I make dinner, I'll tell you that much," Cam replied.

"And you're really good at sports, aren't you, Gabe?" Mrs. E. asked.

Gabe winced. "That might be an overstatement. I like sports. *A lot.*"

Cam patted Gabe on the shoulder and said, "He should give himself more credit. Gabe here is a genius when it comes to analyzing statistics. I'm surprised the NFL or NBA hasn't hired him already."

Even though class hadn't begun yet, Abby raised her hand. She was polite and studious like that. "What have you heard about me?" she asked.

Mrs. E. thought about it for a moment and then asked, "What is 698 times 896?"

Abby didn't even think about it. She immediately said, "625,408. Why?"

Mrs. E. pointed at her. "That's what I know about you. You're a human calculator."

"Actually, she's *the Abacus*," Gabe said.

"Excuse me."

"We call her the Abacus. I gave her that nickname," Gabe said proudly. "Do you know what an abacus is?"

"You mean the world's most ancient type of calculator?" Mrs. E. said, and she reached down onto her desk and picked up a rectangular object. It was around the size of a tablet, but there was no screen. It was simply a wooden frame holding wooden rods laced with wooden beads that could be slid from side to side.

"Is that one ancient?" Cam asked.

Mrs. E. laughed. "No. I bought it a few years ago. I'm not all that great at doing calculations on it, but I love to think about how people have been using these for thousands of years."

As she started to set the abacus back on her

desk, she paused. Her eyes scanned the desk for a moment, and she whispered to herself, "That's odd."

"What's odd?" Abby asked.

"Oh . . . nothing. I think my memory is just playing tricks on me," Mrs. E. said, and she picked the abacus back up. And that's when other students started streaming through the door.

Each time another classmate arrived, Mrs. E. moved the beads on the abacus, which was a way to count them. The students greeted each other with enthusiasm and curiosity. And Mrs. E. greeted them with facts she knew about them. She knew things about everyone, so she wasn't just playing favorites with the Prime Detectives.

After a few minutes, Mrs. E. set her abacus down, shut the door, and said, "Seems we're three students short, but it's time to start the day. And what a day it is. The first day of fourth grade!"

Some kids cheered. A few groaned. Mrs. E. focused on the groaners.

"I think you're gonna love it," she said. "I have a lot of fun things in store for you today. And it will all be capped off by the big bonfire this evening!"

It was an annual tradition to have a bonfire on the first day of school. The fire department supervised as the custodian burned brush and scrap wood left over from the previous year, while kids, teachers, and their families socialized and ate popcorn and ice cream in the fields behind the school. It was a fun way to kick off the year, and nearly every kid looked forward to it.

"I guarantee I'll be there," Cam said.

"Glad to hear it," Mrs. E. said. "How about the rest of—"

Suddenly, the door swung open, and a boy no one recognized jumped into the classroom. He thrust his fist in the air and shouted, "I'm the first one at school!"

He was followed by a second boy, who looked exactly like the first. Not only did he wear the same clothes, but he had the same face!

"And I'm the second!" the second boy said.

A moment after the second boy entered, a third with the same clothes and the same face was jumping in and fist-pumping as well.

"Don't forget the third!" the third boy shouted. "Nothing wrong with third. It's a bronze medal, you know?"

Kids at their desks sat in stunned silence,

and the identical faces of the three boys dropped when they locked eyes with their classmates. That's when Mrs. E. said, "You must be the Penderton triplets. Welcome to Arithmos Elementary School!"

"We're not late, are we?" the first boy asked hesitantly.

"Why is everyone else here before us?" the second boy asked nervously.

"We were supposed to be the first ones at school," the third boy said disappointedly.

All three boys hung their heads. Mrs. E. was still her sunny self, though. "Why don't you each find an open seat?" she said. "Which one of you is Jason?"

The first boy raised his hand, then stomped over to a seat in the back.

"Mason?"

The second boy nodded, then hung his head and sat down next to the first boy.

"Grayson?"

The third boy pointed to himself, sighed, and followed the others.

"I'm sorry you're so disappointed that you were late," Mrs. E. said. "But we're thrilled to have you in class. Everyone, this is Jason, Mason, and Grayson Penderton. They're identical triplets, and they moved to town last week."

"And we spent that whole week planning our big arrival," Jason said with a sigh.

"We practiced eating breakfast, brushing our teeth, and walking here," Mason said with a groan.

"We timed it and everything. We knew exactly how long it would take to get here so that we'd be the first ones at school," Grayson said with a sniffle.

"We didn't want to be late on our first day," all three boys said at the same time.

"So, what happened?" Abby asked.

The three boys threw up their hands. They were utterly clueless.

"Can we see your data set?" Abby asked.

"Our what?" the three boys replied.

"You said you practiced and timed your walks to school," Gabe said. "You must've written down your times. If you have the numbers with you, we can analyze them and see where you went wrong."

"We didn't go wrong," Jason said. "We all had the same time. It took us each thirty-five minutes when we practiced."

Mason checked his watch. "But it took us forty-five minutes today!"

"There's no way we were ten minutes slower than when we practiced," Grayson said.

"Data," Gabe said. "Give us the data."

His tone could've been more polite, but Gabe wasn't often polite. His obsession with facts and figures often made him forget his manners.

"We didn't write it down, but it's easy to remember," Jason said. "When we practiced, it almost always took me fifteen minutes to eat breakfast, six minutes to floss and brush my teeth, and fourteen minutes to walk to school. That adds up to . . ."

"That adds up to thirty-five minutes," Cam said. He didn't need to be as talented as Abby to do a simple calculation like this in his head.

Mason shared his data next. "Twenty minutes to eat breakfast for me, plus two minutes to brush my teeth—flossing is for suckers—and thirteen minutes to walk to school. So, my total is . . ."

"Thirty-five minutes," Cam said again.

"I'm the fastest breakfast-eater at thirteen minutes," Grayson said. "Only three minutes to brush and floss my teeth. And then nineteen minutes to walk to school. When you put that together, you get . . ."

"Thirty-five minutes," Cam said one final time.

Meanwhile, Mrs. E. had been writing the numbers on the whiteboard. It looked like this:

EVIDENCE

Jason: $15 + 6 + 14 = 35$ minutes
Mason: $20 + 2 + 13 = 35$ minutes
Grayson: $13 + 3 + 19 = 35$ minutes

"See!" Jason said, pointing to the board. "It should have taken us thirty-five minutes. Because when we practiced, it took us all thirty-five minutes!"

The class seemed to agree. They all nodded and pointed and whispered things like, "They're right, you know."

"I have a couple questions," Gabe said. "When you timed yourselves, did you each go individually?"

"Of course," Mason said. "We wanted to cheer each other on."

"But this morning, did you wait for each brother to finish his task before moving on to the next one?" Gabe asked.

"Obviously," Grayson said. "We're a team. And we didn't see the point in rushing each other, because we thought it would only take thirty-five minutes."

"When you're a triplet, you don't ever leave your brother behind," Jason said. "Even if you want to sometimes."

"Well, there's your problem right there," Gabe said. "Mrs. E., could you please write one more equation on the board."

"Happily," she said.

"Twenty plus six plus nineteen," Gabe said.

Mrs. E. looked at the class. "Which equals . . ."

"Forty-five!" everyone in the class said at once.

SOLVED

Jason: 15 + 6 + 14 = 35 minutes
Mason: 20 + 2 + 13 = 35 minutes
Grayson: 13 + 3 + 19 = 35 minutes

20 + 6 + 19 = 45 minutes

The faces of the Penderton triplets twisted up in puzzlement.

"Another mystery solved by the Prime Detectives!" Cam announced.

The rest of the class didn't cheer, but they also didn't boo, which was understandable. It was a minor mystery after all.

"What mystery?" Jason asked.

"Yeah, and why was it forty-five?" Mason asked.

"And who the heck are the Prime Detectives?" Grayson asked.

Cam, Gabe, and Abby each took a shot at answering the three questions.

"The mystery was *The Case of the Extra Ten Minutes*," Cam said. "And Gabe found them!"

"As for how I found them and got the answer of forty-five, let me ask you a final question," Gabe said. "Ever heard of buffalo theory?"

The triplets shook their heads.

"Buffalo theory says that a herd of buffalo can only move as fast as their slowest member," Gabe went on. "The same is true for a herd of triplets, especially for ones as loyal to each other as you are. Since you waited for each brother to finish his task before moving on to the next one, we had to put the slowest times for each task in the equation: Mason eating breakfast for twenty minutes, Jason brushing and flossing for six minutes, and Grayson walking to school for nineteen minutes. Adds up to forty-five. Your extra ten minutes."

Recognition lit up the triplets' faces. They were beginning to understand.

"And *we* are the Prime Detectives," Abby told them. "Cam, Gabe, and I. That's what they call us. We're here whenever you need us to solve your trickiest conundrums."

"Well, I'm glad we got that sorted," Mrs. E. said. "But there is one thing about the buffalo theory that Gabe neglected to mention."

"What's that?" Cam asked.

"The only way for the buffalo herd to speed up is for wolves to eat the slowest members." The triplets gulped, and Mrs. E. smiled and added, "So, I hope you can get started earlier tomorrow, fellas."

The class started to laugh, and the triplets started pointing at each other.

"You gotta eat faster," Jason told Mason.

"You gotta brush faster," Grayson told Jason.

"You gotta walk faster," Mason told Grayson.

"And we gotta get this first day started," Mrs. E. said. "Where was I?"

Chapter 2

MRS. E.'S CLASS

In some ways, Mrs. E. was a typical fourth-grade teacher. She taught reading, science, and history. She walked her class to recess and to assemblies. She comforted her students when they were sad or ill, and sent them all postcards whenever she went on vacation. She was good at her job and had been awarded Teacher of the Year on more than one occasion.

In many other ways, Mrs. E. was not a typical fourth-grade teacher. She owned hundreds of different dresses, and they all had unique designs on them. Not just math equations, but reproductions of famous works of art (*The Starry Night*), or optical illusions (Is it a duck, or is it a rabbit?), or quotes from Shakespeare or SpongeBob ("To SquarePants or Not to SquarePants?").

She also rode a hoverboard to school almost every day. On the days she didn't, she rode a unicycle. She wasn't very good at the unicycle, but she was getting better. She considered it a victory whenever she arrived at school without a skinned knee or a bruised elbow. It also taught her students the importance of perseverance.

No day was ever the same in Mrs. E.'s class. For instance, when she taught poetry, she only spoke in rhyme.

"The hour is noon.
I have a hunch,
That very soon,
We'll eat our lunch!"

When there was snow on the ground, Mrs. E. incorporated it into her lessons. Like the time her students made scale-model snowballs to represent our solar system. Earth was the size of a Ping-Pong ball, while Jupiter was the size of a beach ball. And the sun? The sun was a twelve-foot-tall snow boulder that all seventeen kids in class rolled into the middle of the playground.

Cam didn't know if Mrs. E. had something special planned for the first day of school, but he was thrilled when she gave him and the rest of the kids a chance to share their summer adventures. Because Cam had some amazing news to tell the class.

"Welcome, students," Mrs. E. said after the Penderton triplets were seated. "Since we're now all here, I'd love to get started with our morning meeting. Today's theme is 'What have you been up to?' As for me, I spent my summer sailing and reading and relaxing. How about you?"

Cam's hand shot up first, and when Mrs. E. called on him, he said, "I spent my summer getting ready . . . for Netflix!"

A confused hush fell over the class until Mason Penderton asked, "You mean, you're getting a Netflix subscription?"

"We already have a Netflix subscription," his brother Jason said.

"And we didn't even have to get ready for it," their brother Grayson added. "Our parents just had to pay for it."

"He means he's going to be *on* Netflix," Gabe explained with a sigh.

Grayson gasped. "Are you a movie star?"

Cam smiled. "Even better. I'm going to be on *Triumph or Caketastrophe!*"

He jumped up from his seat when he said

Caketastrophe and spread his arms in glory. A few kids smiled or raised their eyebrows at the information, but Abby was the most enthusiastic, clapping and whistling in support of her friend.

"Maybe not everyone in class knows what *Triumph or Caketastrophe* is," Mrs. E. said. "Do you mind telling us?"

Cam rolled his eyes. "It's merely the greatest baking and obstacle course competition show for children between the ages of nine and twelve."

"Baking *and* an obstacle course?" Mrs. E. asked. "How does that work?"

"Simple," Abby explained. "The contestants are assigned ingredients, then they have to carry all the ingredients through an obstacle course. If they drop any, they can't use them. When they get to the end of the course, they arrive at a kitchen where they bake something with whatever ingredients they have left over. Then they've gotta carry their baked item back through the obstacle course. Whatever remains is what the judges eat. Plus, you get extra points for going fast."

"Sounds exciting," Mrs. E. said.

"It's beyond exciting!" Abby proclaimed. "It's stupendous! And it's my favorite show. I'm so proud that Cam is going to be on it."

"Well, it's not as exciting as college football," Gabe said. "But it's still an entertaining way to spend thirty minutes."

"And Gabe and Abby have been helping me get ready," Cam said. "We've been building obstacle courses, and they've been teaching me about measurements."

"But you're a cook, right?" Mrs. E. asked. "Don't cooks already know about measurements?"

"I'm a cook but not a baker," Cam explained. "There's a difference. Cooking is more instinctual. I learned to cook through my senses. I rarely use recipes because I can sense what a dish needs."

"How so?" Mrs. E. asked.

"Easy," Cam said. "Need to know if your oil is hot enough to fry potatoes? Look at its shimmer and listen to the sizzle. Want to know if a steak is ready? Press it with a finger to see how soft it is. Worried that your soup doesn't have the right seasonings? Give it a sniff. Or better yet, taste it, silly! But with baking, you can't do those things. Your measurements have to be exact. Then you have to trust the oven to do its job. Baking is closer to a science. And it's a science I'm still learning."

"Very interesting," Mrs. E. said. "And you'll have to tell us when we can watch the show."

"Oh, don't worry," Gabe told everyone. "If Cam does *anything*, you'll hear about it."

Cam shrugged his shoulders and said, "Probably true. I'm not shy."

"We're not shy, either," Jason Penderton said as he stood up from his desk.

"Which is why we wanted to be the first ones to school today," his brother Mason said as he stood up, too.

"Because we have something special to share with the entire class," Grayson said as he stood up as well. He also reached into his backpack and pulled out a large plastic bag.

The bag wasn't clear, so no one could see what was inside.

"Is it video games?" a kid named Maisie asked.

"No."

"Is it puppies?" a kid named Sanjeev asked.

"No."

"Is it cookies?" Abby asked.

The triplets' faces dropped, and then Grayson reached into the plastic bag and pulled out a very large and very round chocolate chip cookie. "How did you know it was cookies?" he asked.

"Is there really anything more to life than video games, puppies, and cookies?" Abby asked.

There wasn't. At least not for these kids. Therefore, no one objected.

"Thank you for being so generous," Mrs. E. said. "But perhaps we can wait until we've finished our morning meeting before we dive in to any snacks."

"Yes, ma'am," Grayson said, and returned the cookie to the bag. Then the triplets sat back down.

For the rest of the morning, other students took the spotlight, talking about their summers.

Maisie told the class about all the camps she had attended, including art camp, horseback-riding camp, and cave diving camp.

"Did I hear you right?" Mrs. E. asked. "Did you say cave diving?"

"Yes," Maisie said. "Underwater spelunking. It's super awesome and super scary at the same time. Simply perfect."

Sanjeev's summer was not simply perfect. "My lemonade stand didn't turn the profit I had hoped," he said with a sigh.

"How much did you make?" Mrs. E. asked.

"After building expenses, ingredients, and

marketing, I made around seventeen cents," he said.

You didn't have to be a math genius to know that seventeen cents' profit was not much of a profit.

More kids described their summers. Kiko went to the beach and went camping. Emmett did a lot of mountain biking and reading. Luciana helped around the house while her parents took care of her new baby brother. She also invented a water-balloon cannon.

The Prime Detectives already knew many of their fellow fourth graders, but it was nice to learn more about them and hear about their summers. When it came time for the Penderton triplets to

talk about their summer, they enthusiastically described a vacation spent on their grandparents' farm where they learned to take care of chickens, harvest corn, and . . .

"Bake triple chocolate chip cookies!" all three announced.

"We made them from our grandma's recipe," Mason said.

"They're extra delicious," Jason said.

"And everyone knows that kids are better students when they are well-fed," Grayson said. "Especially when they're fed chocolate chip cookies."

"Okay, okay," Mrs. E. said with a laugh. "You win. You can share them now."

The three boys pumped their fists and then gleefully started removing the cookies from the bag. The cookies were enormous (around the size of a small plate), so one per student was more than enough. And they had exactly eighteen cookies. One for each of the seventeen students, plus Mrs. E.

"Before everyone eats their cookies, we'd like to say that we really enjoyed hearing what you did over the summer," Grayson said as he and his brothers started passing the treats around.

"And we look forward to getting to know you better," Jason said.

"Arithmos Elementary seems like a great school full of great kids and a great teacher," Mason said.

This made everyone in the room smile, which prompted the triplets to call out at the same time. "Bon appétit!"

And the class dug in.

For a moment, the only sounds were of crunching and chewing. But the sounds quickly changed. First there were some contemplative *hmms*. And then there were some questioning *huhs*. Next there were disgusted *ughs*. And spitting. And retching. And finally yelling.

"The cookies! The cookies!" Luciana screamed as she ran toward the front of the class.

"What?" Mrs. E. said as she raised her unbitten cookie to her mouth.

But she couldn't take a bite because Luciana slapped the cookie from her hand and screamed, "They're poisonous!"

Chapter 3

THE CASE OF THE POISONOUS COOKIES

Luciana wasn't the only kid worried about the cookies. Maisie ran across the room and spit her bite into a trash can. Sanjeev threw his half-eaten cookie out the open window. Cam simply licked and sniffed his cookie and then held it up to the light to give it a closer look.

The Penderton triplets were aghast. That means they were horrified and confused. Or at least, that's how they were acting. They were scurrying around the room, waving their arms back and forth as if a false alarm had sounded.

"They're not poisonous," Jason assured his new classmates. "They're not poisonous!"

"They're very delicious," Mason added. "The most delicious cookies ever! And even better when served with chocolate milk."

Then Grayson took a bite of his cookie to prove this. But his face went sour. "Um . . . actually . . . maybe not the *most* delicious."

"Just say it," Gabe told them. "They're awful!"

The rest of the class agreed with *uh-huhs* and *yeps* and nodding heads. There wasn't a single person who tasted the cookie and liked what they had tasted.

"I don't get it," Jason said. "Grandma's recipe is perfect."

"We've been eating these our whole lives," Mason said.

"They've never tasted like this before," Grayson said.

"Maybe because you weren't trying to poison people before!" Luciana shouted.

Mrs. E. stood up and motioned for everyone to sit down. "Let's stay calm for a moment. Clearly this is a misunderstanding."

"A misunderstanding of how to read a recipe," Gabe said.

"We didn't read it," Grayson said. "We have it memorized."

"Cool," Abby said. "You must have good Memory Palaces."

The triplets scratched at their heads until Mason asked, "Memory Palaces? Do you mean our brains? Because that's where we remember things. I guess our brains are good."

Abby shrugged. "I don't mean your brains exactly. I mean the part of your brains where you keep the stuff you want to remember. Your Memory Palaces."

She said it like everyone should've known what she was talking about, but the class clearly didn't have a clue. The room was full of blank stares until Mrs. E. explained.

"Abby is referring to an old memorization technique," Mrs. E. told them. "It's called the Memory Palace. But it's also known as *loci*. It's simple. When you want to remember something, you imagine a large building. A palace, for instance. Then you take all the things you're trying to remember, and you imagine objects that remind you of those things. You put the objects in different rooms of the palace. That way, when you need to remember things, you can simply imagine walking through the palace from room to room and seeing the objects. You can memorize a lot of things this way, and often in a very specific order."

Abby pointed at Mrs. E. and said, "That. That's exactly what I do. Doesn't everyone do that?"

"I sometimes make up songs or poems to remember things," a kid named Noah said.

"That's an example of rhyming technique," Mrs. E. said. "And that's a good one, too. But let's look closer at the Memory Palace because I think it's quite helpful for learning. Everyone close their eyes for a moment, and I'll describe how I might remember the triplets' names."

The kids all closed their eyes, and the room became very quiet.

"Now, your Memory Palace might be a giant palace if you need to remember a lot of things," Mrs. E. said. "Or, if you need to remember just a few things, it might be something smaller. For this exercise, my Memory Palace is going to be my house. And I will start in my kitchen. Let's say I want to remember Mason's name first. Maybe I'll place an object on the kitchen counter. It can be anything that's a reminder of Mason. How about a mason jar?"

"I'm imagining a calendar on the wall with the month of May on it. There's a Sunday circled, so that's how I remember the sounds *may* and *sun*," Sanjeev said.

"Perfect," Mrs. E. said. "Okay, so next I'm imagining that I'm moving out of the kitchen and into the dining room. That's where I find a gravy boat on the dining room table. The sound of the word *gravy* reminds me of Grayson."

"I see a painting on the wall," Maisie said. "It's of the sun, but it's not yellow. It's gray. A gray sun!"

"Even better than mine!" Mrs. E. exclaimed. "You're all so good at this. My final stop is going to be in the living room where I'll see a birdcage. In that birdcage there are two blue jays: a big one and a little one. The big one is the father, and the little one is the son. The jay's son. Now I've remembered Jason."

"All I see is a big, poisonous, chocolate chip cookie," Luciana said.

"It wasn't poisonous!" Jason shouted.

And then all the kids opened their eyes and started talking at the same time, complaining about the cookies and shattering their Memory Palaces.

"Okay, okay, okay," Mrs. E. said, waving her arms. "Let's talk about those cookies. Which I am sure are not poisonous. Let's figure out what happened. Perhaps the Pendertons didn't remember the recipe correctly, and that's why the cookies don't taste the way they should. Remembering three names is easy, especially using the Memory Palace technique. But memorizing a recipe with a lot of different ingredients in different amounts can be hard."

"Half a cup of butter, softened," Jason said confidently. "Half a cup of white sugar. Half a cup of packed brown sugar."

"One egg," Mason said even more confidently. "One teaspoon of vanilla extract. One and a half cups of flour."

"Half a teaspoon of salt," Grayson said with the most confidence. "Half a teaspoon of baking soda. And one and a third cups of semisweet chocolate chips, milk chocolate chips, and dark chocolate chips combined."

"And that's what you need to make our grandma's triple chocolate chip cookies," the triplets said at the same time.

Mrs. E. was silent for a moment and then she clapped her hands lightly, as if she were at the ballet. "Bravo. I'm impressed by your memories."

"And I'm impressed by the recipe, because those actually sound like pretty good cookies," Cam said, and then he held his cookie up. "But they're not this cookie."

"Interesting," Abby said. "Do you think someone maybe switched the cookies on you?"

"Impossible," Jason said. "We baked them last night, let them cool, and then packed them immediately afterward. No one else had access to our bags."

"Maybe someone dripped poison on them while you were sleeping," Gabe said. "How much do you trust your parents?"

"Our parents didn't poison the cookies," Mason said angrily.

"No one poisoned the cookies," Jason added.

"Why would anyone poison the cookies?" Grayson asked.

Nobody in class had a good answer to that, probably because calling the cookies poisonous was bad enough, but accusing someone of poisoning them on purpose was perhaps too much.

Cam didn't make accusations. He asked

questions. "I'm wondering if you can tell me some things," he said to the triplets.

"Sure, what do you need to know?" Jason asked.

"Have you ever made this many cookies before?"

The boys shook their heads. "We usually just bake them for ourselves," Jason said.

"Makes sense." Cam asked, "But when you decided to make more cookies, what sort of arithmetic did you use?"

"Well, we had to divide the cookies up, right?" Jason said. "So, I used division."

"Subtraction, too," Mason said. "Because you have to subtract the smaller number of cookies from the bigger number. That's how you know the difference."

"Interesting," Cam said. "And when it comes to conversions, can you tell me how many tablespoons there are in a cup?"

"Sixteen," Jason said. "I think."

"That sounds right, but I'd have to check," Mason asked.

"I'm pretty sure it's a lot fewer than sixteen," Grayson said. "I think it's four."

"Got it," Cam said. "Those are great answers and all I need to know."

"Really?" Gabe said.

"I believe the triplets," Cam announced to the class. "And I believe they used the right recipe. Or at least they thought they did. And I believe the cookies were never poisoned. I'll prove it."

Then Cam lifted the cookie to his mouth, and he took a huge bite. With a full mouth, he mumbled something about flour ratio.

The class gasped.

What was he thinking?

He chewed the cookie for a moment, and while it didn't look like he was enjoying it, he was definitely taking his time with it. He seemed to be thinking about it. And he said something to himself that sounded like *sweetness factor*.

He took another bite, swallowed, and whispered, "Hmm . . . baking soda-y."

More gasps from the class. More thinking from Cam. And another bite.

Was he out of his mind?

He kept biting and thinking, and the class kept gasping and wondering.

Until finally, Cam had eaten the entire cookie. He picked up his water bottle, took a long swig from it, and announced, "I've solved the mystery."

36

In many ways, Cam was an ordinary kid. His tongue, however, was far from ordinary. It was, quite simply, extraordinary. And it wasn't because it was strangely long or round or twisty.

It was because it could differentiate between so many different flavors, far more than the average tongue. This might've seemed like a curse because it meant most of his eating experiences were intense.

For instance, lemonade was extra puckery, and broccoli tasted extra broccoli-ish. But Cam liked intense eating experiences. Even ones where the food didn't taste very good. *Why?* Because he liked learning.

So, in a certain way, he liked eating the Penderton triplets' disgusting triple chocolate chip cookie. It was an education, a journey, a path to unraveling a mystery.

"You told me that you usually make these cookies for yourselves," Cam said to the triplets. "So, does that recipe you memorized only make three cookies?"

"Three *giant* cookies," Mason said.

"One for each of us," Grayson said.

"Our grandma likes to be fair," Jason said.

"But you brought cookies for the entire class and Mrs. E.," Cam said. "So how many cookies is that in total?"

"Eighteen," the three boys said at the same time.

"Right," Cam said. "It's clear what you did wrong then."

"How could you possibly know that?" Jason asked.

"Yeah," Grayson said. "You weren't looking in our window, were you?"

"Because that would be very creepy," Mason said.

"I'm with you there, my friend," Cam said. "That would be creepy indeed. But no, I didn't look in your window. I learned everything I need to know from what you told me. And from tasting your cookie."

"Enlighten us, Cam," Mrs. E. said. "What did you learn?"

"I learned that the triplets each measured a different group of ingredients."

"How do you mean?" Mrs. E. asked.

"One of them measured the butter, white sugar, and brown sugar," Cam said.

"He's right," Jason said. "I did."

"One of them measured the eggs, vanilla extract, and the flour."

"That'd be me," Mason said.

"And one of them measured the salt, baking soda, and chocolate chips."

"I'm your guy," Grayson said.

Mrs. E., who had been searching through her desk drawers for something, looked up for a moment and asked Cam, "How did you know that?"

"No worries," Cam said. "I'm getting there. May I use the whiteboard for a moment?"

"Of course," Mrs. E. said as she pushed the desk drawers shut.

"Great," Cam said as he walked to the front of the room. "I'll need some assistance from Gabe and Abby, because while I know what the triplets did wrong, I often make mistakes in my calculations. They'll check them for me."

"Happy to help," Abby said, joining Cam up front.

"If I must," Gabe grumbled as he did, too.

"So," Cam said, "when you have a recipe that's for three cookies, and you want to make eighteen cookies, you need to change the amount of ingredients in that recipe, right?"

The class agreed with nods.

"You need to multiply the ingredients," Cam went on. "In the case of this recipe, it's a pretty simple conversion. All you gotta do is divide the eighteen cookies you need for the class by the three cookies each recipe makes. You'll figure out that you need six times as many ingredients."

Gabe put two representations of the equation on the whiteboard. First, he wrote:

EVIDENCE

$$18 \div 3 = 6$$

Then he drew six separate groups of three circles, showing all eighteen cookies.

"Jason, who was measuring the butter and the sugars, understood the equation that you see on the board," Cam said.

"That's true," Jason said. "I divided eighteen by three and got six."

"Buuuut," Cam continued, "Jason didn't multiply his ingredients by six. His head was stuck in division mode. So, he divided his ingredients by six. Half a cup of butter and half a cup of the white and brown sugars became . . ."

Gabe wrote the equation on the whiteboard.

$$\frac{1}{2} \div 6 \ (\text{or} \ \frac{1}{2} \times \frac{1}{6}) = \frac{1}{12} = \ \text{4 TEASPOONS}$$
CUP   CUP   CUP   CUP   EACH OF BUTTER AND SUGAR

 NOT ENOUGH BUTTER, WHITE SUGAR, AND BROWN SUGAR

"One twelfth of a cup," Abby said. "Or a measly four teaspoons of each."

Jason nodded. "It did seem a little weird at the time to be using such a small amount of everything."

Mason shook his head in disgust. "How could you make that mistake? It was obvious that you had to multiply."

"For some people maybe," Cam said. "But you're not innocent here, either, my friend. Because you made your own mistake."

"What?" Mason said. "Impossible. I multiplied. I didn't divide."

"Yes, but you didn't multiply by the right number

because you didn't divide in the beginning. You subtracted."

"Right," Mason said. "I wanted to know the difference between a recipe for eighteen cookies and one for three."

"So, you subtracted three from eighteen and got fifteen, right?" Cam asked.

"Right."

"But that's fifteen. You multiplied by fifteen! And one egg, one teaspoon of vanilla extract, and one and a half cups of flour became . . ."

"Fifteen eggs, five tablespoons of vanilla extract, and a whopping twenty-two and a half cups of flour," Abby said.

Once again, Gabe jotted the equation on the board.

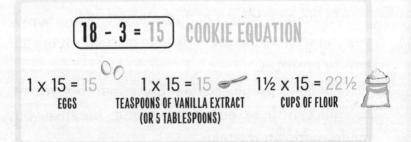

(18 - 3 = 15) COOKIE EQUATION

1 x 15 = 15   1 x 15 = 15   1½ x 15 = 22½
EGGS   TEASPOONS OF VANILLA EXTRACT   CUPS OF FLOUR
        (OR 5 TABLESPOONS)

"That's way too much," Grayson told his brother, and Mason hung his head in shame.

"Not so fast, triplet number three, because you messed up, too," Cam said.

"No, I didn't," Grayson said. "I divided eighteen by three to get six, and then I multiplied my ingredients by six. Just like I was supposed to do."

"True," Cam said. "But your problem is a problem that I share. I don't always remember the correct conversions of measurements. Abby does, of course. So, let's test her." Cam turned to his friend. "Abby, how many teaspoons are in a tablespoon?"

"Three," Abby said.

"How many tablespoons in a quarter cup?"

"Four."

"How many quarter cups in a cup?"

"Four."

"How many cups in a pint?"

"Two."

"How many pints in a quart?"

"Two."

"How many quarts in a gallon?"

"Four."

"So, if you know all that, then you must know how many teaspoons there are in a gallon, right?"

"Seven hundred and sixty-eight," Abby said almost as soon as Cam finished asking.

Gabe wrote the conversions and the equation out on the board and checked a calculator. Though he didn't need to, because Abby was never wrong.

"Perfect, as always," he announced.

CONVERSION CHART		
3 TEASPOONS	=	1 TABLESPOON
4 TABLESPOONS	=	¼ CUP
4 QUARTER CUPS	=	1 CUP
2 CUPS	=	1 PINT
2 PINTS	=	1 QUART
4 QUARTS	=	1 GALLON

$$3 \times 4 \times 4 \times 2 \times 2 \times 4 = 768 \text{ TEASPOONS IN A GALLON}$$

"Okay," Cam said. "Now let's get back to Grayson. When Grayson multiplied his ingredients, he multiplied his half teaspoons of salt and baking soda by six and should've ended up with . . ."

"Three teaspoons," Abby said. "Which converts to one tablespoon of each."

$$\frac{1}{2} \times 6 = 3 \quad \longrightarrow \quad \text{3 TEASPOONS}$$
TEASPOON   TEASPOONS   (OR 1 TABLESPOON OF EACH)

"But I'm betting Grayson added a quarter cup of each, instead of a tablespoon of each," Cam said.

"Why would he do that?" Gabe asked.

"Because he got his conversions mixed up," Cam said. "He thought that there were three teaspoons in a quarter cup."

"You mean there aren't?" Grayson asked quietly.

Cam pointed to the conversions on the whiteboard. "Nope. You can see there are three teaspoons in a *tablespoon*. But there are four *tablespoons* in a quarter cup. You skipped right over that tablespoon conversion."

"I see that now," Grayson said with a sigh.

"Then you mixed the conversions up the other way when you measured out the chocolate chips and didn't put in nearly enough," Cam went on. "You did the calculation correctly, and multiplied one and a third cups by six to get . . ."

"Eight cups," Abby said. "Which is also four pints, or two quarts, or half a gallon."

"That's a lot of chocolate chips," Cam said. "But you added only one pint of chocolate chips to the mix, didn't you?"

Grayson shrugged and admitted, "Yeah. I thought there were eight cups in a pint."

"There are eight *pints* in a *gallon*, so I can see how you'd get mixed up," Cam said. "I get mixed up, too. Also, measuring pints and quarts and gallons is usually for liquid measurements. It's best to stick to cups for dry measurements, no matter how large the number. Or better yet, skip cups altogether and weigh your ingredients. For things like baking, using the weight is much more precise."

"Thank you, that's helpful," Jason said. "But there's one thing still confusing me. You weren't spying on us, but you knew exactly what we did with our cookies. How?"

"When I asked you those questions, you hinted at your arithmetic mistakes," Cam said.

"But you knew everything about the specific ingredients," Mason said.

"We didn't tell you who measured what," Grayson said.

Cam stuck out his tongue and tapped it. "You didn't have to. I have extra tastebuds. I'm a supertaster. Which means I could tell that your cookies were not sweet or buttery enough. But they were also too vanilla-flavored, too soda-y, too eggy, and way too salty. I didn't even need my tastebuds for the chocolate chips. Just look at those things. They're called triple chocolate chip cookies but there are barely any chocolate chips in 'em."

"We thought they looked weird," Jason said with a sigh. "But we also thought we were being too critical of ourselves. We were nervous for today."

"We really wanted to make a good impression," Grayson said with a groan.

"But we ruined it," Mason said with a sniffle.

"The only thing you ruined was a batch of cookies," Mrs. E. said. "And cookies can be made again. But can I offer you a suggestion?"

"Yes, ma'am," the triplets said.

"Next time, taste your cookies before you share them."

THE ORIGINAL RECIPE FOR TRIPLE CHOCOLATE CHIP COOKIES

Yield: makes three large cookies

Ingredients: organized by triplet

Jason

½ cup butter, softened

½ cup white sugar

½ cup packed brown sugar

Mason

1 egg

1 teaspoon vanilla extract

1½ cups all-purpose flour

Grayson

½ teaspoon salt

½ teaspoon baking soda

1 ⅓ cups mixed semisweet, milk, and dark chocolate chips

Heat oven to 375°F. In a small bowl, mix flour, baking soda, and salt.

In a large bowl, beat butter, white sugar, and brown sugar until fluffy. Then beat in egg and vanilla.

Add flour mixture from small bowl to large bowl and mix until combined. Stir in chocolate chips.

Separate dough into three equal pieces. Form each piece into a ball. Flatten each ball on an ungreased cookie sheet until it's approximately a half-inch thick. Space the cookies on the sheet so that they don't touch each other.

Bake for 15–20 minutes, or until a toothpick inserted in the center of each cookie comes out clean.

Let cookies cool for 10 minutes on cookie sheet. Then place cookies on wire rack to cool for an additional 30 minutes.

Chapter 4

FIRST DAYS

First days at Arithmos Elementary were usually exciting enough, with the new teachers and the yearly bonfire. But the late arrival of the Penderton triplets and their absolutely terrible cookies had set the fourth grade ablaze with chatter. Many of their classmates spent the entire morning trying to figure the Pendertons out.

Where are they from?
Why are they here?
What's their deal?

Gabe wasn't necessarily in the market for three new friends, and he *was* a naturally suspicious person, but he trusted that the data told him all he needed to know about the triplets. The *deal* with the Pendertons, as far as he was concerned, was that they were three mostly friendly and rather goofy kids who were terrible at math. Nothing more and nothing less.

"They seem harmless," Gabe said as he, Abby, and Cam made their way out of the classroom. "Just don't cheat off them during math quizzes."

"Or use them as sous-chefs," Cam added.

"What's a sous-chef?" Abby asked.

"It's the chef who's the assistant to the head chef," Cam said. "They make sure the kitchen is running smoothly and correctly."

"Yeah," Abby said. "They might not be so good at that."

"Do you get any sous-chefs on *Triumph or Caketastrophe?*" Gabe asked.

"That would be called a pastry chef, or pâtissier," Cam said. "And no. I'm flying solo. Which reminds me, we need to practice a new obstacle course."

"Already on it," Gabe said. "Abby and I plotted it out yesterday. We can show you during recess."

"Can't wait," Cam replied.

Neither could Gabe. But as they walked into the hall toward the music classroom, he had another concern. Particularly the piece of paper that was stuck to his shoe.

"What's this?" he asked as he peeled it off his sole.

The paper was white, but it had a dark sticky stain on it, and someone had written something in black marker.

128IN3

"It looks like a license plate number," Cam said.

"Well, I don't drive, so why should I care?" Gabe said.

He was about to throw the paper out when Abby snatched it from his hand. "I'll recycle it later," she said, and she folded it up and put it in her pocket.

"Fine by me," Gabe said. "Only thing on my mind right now is my obstacle course."

Helping Cam train for the show had been the highlight of Gabe's summer. There was little that Gabe loved more than competition but, unfortunately, he was struggling as an athlete. Gabe was tiny, slow, and uncoordinated.

He tried as hard as he could, but when he was on the soccer field or the baseball diamond or the basketball court, other kids usually dominated. That didn't stop him from playing, though. He knew he would grow. He knew he would get better with practice. Even if he never caught up with his peers, he knew he would always love playing sports.

The one thing Gabe loved more than playing sports was analyzing them, something he didn't need to be big or fast or strong to do. He only needed to be dedicated and smart. Luckily, he was both. After games, he'd go over statistics with his teammates to tell them what they did well and what they could do better. Coaches would sometimes hand him their clipboards and say things like, *Maybe you should take my job.* And they'd only be half-joking.

Therefore, coaching Cam was a thrill for Gabe. But he tried not to be emotional about it because he knew his job was to be analytical.

"I've been crunching the numbers, and you should be able to complete the new obstacle course in around one and a half minutes. And I think you can improve that time by around two seconds per day if you train consistently," Gabe said.

"How many days until the show?" Abby asked.

"Seventy-two," Cam said.

"Cool," Abby said. "If you improve by two seconds a day, you'll be going backward in time by then!"

Gabe grumbled. "Fine. He'll hit a plateau at a certain point and probably won't be able to improve on his PR, but if he listens to me, he'll get as far as humanly possible."

"What's my PR?" Cam asked. "My *papas rellenas?*"

"Huh?" Gabe said.

"*Papas rellenas,*" Cam said again. "They're Cuban stuffed potatoes, and they're delicious. You should try them sometime."

Gabe shook his head and sighed. "I'm talking about your *personal record*. All competitive people keep track of their PRs."

"Oh," Cam said. "I don't. But that's what you're around for. To keep track of mine."

Other kids might have looked at this as an insult. To Gabe, it was simply part of the job. "True," he said. "But you do realize that I have a lot of other things to keep track of as well. I'm the official statistician for the high school boy's football, basketball, and baseball teams this year."

"We know," Cam said. "You have the T-shirt."

The T-shirt Cam was referring to was white with blue lettering that read: OFFICIAL STATISTICIAN. Gabe knew

which T-shirt he was referring to, because Gabe was currently wearing that T-shirt. He washed it and wore it nearly every day.

Abby pointed to the T-shirt and said, "Since you hang out with high school kids all time, maybe you can find out which ones are good at chess. Or calculus. Or differential equations. No one in fourth grade wants to talk about differential equations."

"Because no one in fourth grade knows what differential equations are!" Cam cried.

"I do," Abby said with a shrug. "They're fun."

All of a sudden, the Penderton triplets pushed past the three Prime Detectives. "You know what's really fun?" Mason said as he bulldozed into the music room.

"Making music!" Jason hollered, following him.

Then Grayson surged ahead of his brothers until he found a bongo drum, and he immediately began to slap a steady beat. Mason joined him by shaking a maraca, and Jason played a little tune on a recorder. They weren't bad.

Abby laughed. "At least you can't accuse them of being boring."

Music was as fun as it ever was. It helped that Mr. Lopez was a fantastic music teacher, and even kids who weren't great singers or musicians could find some way to shine in his class.

The Pendertons turned out to be quite talented musicians and continued to amuse and puzzle their new classmates. They seemed like nice kids, and ones who really enjoyed school, but many of their fellow fourth graders were still suspicious of them. *Were they simply struggling at math? Or was something more sinister afoot?*

Reading class was next, and while Mrs. E. was as enthusiastic as ever—particularly when she introduced the class to a new series of books about a walrus who was also a wizard (aka Wizard Walrus!)—she also seemed a bit distracted.

All her free moments were spent peeking in desks and behind bookshelves, as if she were looking for something. Whatever it was, she didn't seem to find it, though one of the Penderton triplets offered some unhelpful advice: "You should try looking wherever you left it."

Gym class was next, and Gabe was impressed by the Pendertons' enthusiasm, though not by their physical prowess. During kickball, all three kicked as hard as they could. And all three missed the ball.

The gym teacher, Mr. Largo, gave the triplets a quick tour of the gym and the equipment closet after class while the rest of the students went to lunch.

That meant that the Prime Detectives couldn't keep a close eye on them, which was a shame. Not that they were suspicious of the Pendertons. It was more because the triplets were fascinating.

They didn't have the shyness that other new kids possessed. Gabe could attest to that. He had been a new kid exactly one year before.

The first day of third grade had been terrifying for Gabe. He had moved to town two weeks before and hadn't met a single kid yet. In his old school, he had a few good friends, and plenty of kids he played sports with, but he had never started over like this.

The entire morning, he only said a handful of words. And while kids weren't mean to him, very few talked to him. He was okay with that for the most part. He didn't like being the center of attention. But he also didn't like being lonely.

So, when he sat down alone at lunch on that first day, and a broad-shouldered boy with a big smile and dark curls sat down next to him, Gabe didn't tell him he didn't want to be alone. But he also didn't speak to the boy. Which didn't matter. The boy was happy to comment on Gabe's lunch anyway.

"Some nice choices there," Cam said, pointing to Gabe's bean burrito, carrot sticks, and fruit gummies. "And better than today's cafeteria offerings. The lunch workers are wonderful people, but they do not know how to craft a proper pulled pork sandwich. No way, no how. My advice is to skip that whenever it's on the menu."

Gabe looked up from his burrito. "Thanks," he said.

"No problemo," Cam said. "My name is Cam. I already know yours is Gabe because I always know the new kids' names. It's one of my things. This is one of my things, too."

Cam slid a paper bag over to Gabe.

"What's in it?" Gabe asked.

"Homemade potato chips," Cam said. "With my own special seasoning. Tastier and healthier than the store-bought stuff. Give 'em a whirl."

Gabe pulled one out of the bag. He looked at it. He sniffed it. He touched it to his tongue. It seemed safe enough. So, he crunched it. And . . .

"Wow," Gabe said. "These are really good."

"Thanks," Cam replied. "They're all yours. I've got around twenty bags in my backpack. Never know when someone else will have a craving."

"I have a craving," said a tall girl with three tight ponytails and rainbow-colored braces. She immediately sat down next to them.

"Hey, Abby," Cam said, reaching into his backpack and grabbing a bag of chips for her. "Have you met Gabe yet? He's new."

"Hi, Gabe," Abby said. "Welcome to Arithmos Elementary."

"Thanks," Gabe said again.

"What sorts of things are you into, Gabe?" Abby asked.

"I like sports," Gabe said.

"Cool, so do I," Abby said. "Check out this sport. Cam, do you have a stopwatch?"

Cam pointed to a purple device on his wrist. "My Fitbit does."

"Okay, time me," Abby said, and she lifted her bag of chips.

Cam started the stopwatch, and Abby began eating. She practically inhaled the chips, and when she was done, she slammed her palms on the table and cried, "Time!"

"8.67 seconds," Cam announced.

"Since there were twenty-one chips in my bag, that means it took me on average 0.41285714285 seconds per chip."

Gabe was flabbergasted by the speed of Abby's calculations. "Is that true?" he asked.

"Probably," Cam said.

"How is that possible?" Gabe asked.

"It wasn't that hard, actually," Abby said. "You simply have to know the most popular cyclical number in the base ten system. I'll teach you sometime."

"I don't know what any of that means, but yes, please do teach me," Gabe said. "Before that, though, I have to beat your record. Cam, get your stopwatch ready."

And as Gabe lifted his bag of chips toward his mouth, he realized he had found two new friends.

Lunch on the first day of fourth grade wasn't much different. In fact, in one way, it was exactly the same. Abby, Cam, and Gabe were about to have another potato chip–eating race, but before they could even start, Mrs. E. approached them.

"How's lunch going, gang?" Mrs. E. asked.

"About to get a lot more exciting," Cam said. "We're starting a new season of the Chip Olympics. The time to beat is currently 6.28 seconds. I'm the world record holder."

"That does sound exciting," Mrs. E. said. "And I don't want to keep you from it, but I have a question for the three of you. You were the first students in the classroom this morning. Did any of you see my iPad anywhere?"

The three kids looked at each other and then shook their heads.

"It's missing?" Abby asked.

"Seems to be," Mrs. E. said. "I swear I left it on my desk yesterday afternoon after I set up the classroom for today. But this morning it was gone."

"Oh, dear," Cam said. "Was the door locked?"

"I locked it when I left at 3:00 p.m.," Mrs. E. said. "And unlocked it this morning right before you arrived at 8:00 a.m."

"Sounds like another mystery to me," Gabe said.

"Whatever it is, I'd like it back," Mrs. E. said. "So, if you see it, let me know. Its case is covered in shiny rhinestones. You won't be able to miss it."

Mrs. E. gave them a little wave and moved on to the next table, where she appeared to be asking other fourth graders the same question. She even spoke to the Penderton triplets, interrupting them as they poured chocolate milk from a large plastic jug into three separate plastic cups.

The Prime Detectives couldn't hear what Mrs. E. was saying, but they could see the triplets shaking their heads, and they could make out the disappointed look on Mrs. E.'s face.

"I think she's really upset that she lost that iPad," Cam said.

"They're worth a lot of money," Gabe said.

"And maybe she has important things saved on it," Abby said.

"And it's even better at calculations than an abacus," Gabe said.

Abby cleared her throat theatrically.

"You think you could beat an actual computer?" Gabe asked.

Abby shrugged. "I never tried."

"Well, you're going to have to try later," Cam said. "Recess is in a few minutes, and that means it's obstacle course time."

Chapter 5

THE CASE OF
THE ZIP LINE DISASTER

Gabe walked Cam through the obstacle course. It began at the monkey bars. That was enough to make Cam want to throw in the towel.

"I can't even do *one* of those," Cam said.

"You'll be able to do them all in no time," Gabe said. "Trust me. And some of the stuff here is much harder than what you'll face on the actual show, so you'll be more prepared than anyone."

The route moved to the climbing dome, then to the structure with the twisty slide, back to the climbing dome, over to the seesaw, across the sandbox, through the tire swing, back to the monkey bars, up the firefighter's pole, and then finally to the zip line.

"A zip line I can do," Cam said. "And since

I'm heavier than most kids, I'll be even faster. Simple physics."

"True," Gabe said. "But there's a wrinkle in this part."

"A wrinkle?" Cam said.

"We're going to throw foam balls at you while you zip," Abby said.

"Yikes," Cam said.

"It won't hurt," Gabe assured him. "It will mostly be a distraction."

"What if I fall off and bump my tailbone?" Cam asked.

"There's ice for that," Gabe said with a shrug.

"How many balls are we talking about?" Cam asked.

Gabe pointed to three buckets a few yards away, each overflowing with balls.

"That's . . . a lot," Cam said. "How will you throw them all?"

"That's the best part," Abby said. "Everyone in class is gonna help!"

That's when Cam noticed something. All the kids in his class were standing near the buckets. Many of them had smiles on their faces. Fiendish smiles.

"Oh my goodness gracious," Cam said.

"You don't want to let them down," Gabe said. "Why not give it a try?"

Some of their classmates must have been listening in, because Cam noticed many of the smiling kids were now nodding.

Cam had to admit it sounded kind of fun, like something an action hero would do. The ground below the zip line was soft mulch, so falling wouldn't be too bad really, even if he bumped his tailbone. As for the balls? Honestly, how much would a bunch of foam balls hurt?

"All right, I'll try it," Cam said.

"The whole obstacle course?" Gabe asked.

Cam laughed. "Let's start with the zip line and then work our way on to the stuff where I actually have to do something other than be a foam-ball target."

The kids who had smiled and nodded were now pumping their fists and walking over to the buckets and filling their hands, pockets, and shirts with balls. The balls were around the size of baseballs or tennis balls and came in a variety of colors and designs. Some even looked like baseballs or tennis balls because they were designed for practicing inside where they wouldn't break windows . . . or bones.

Cam walked confidently over to the zip line. He had ridden it countless times during his years at Arithmos Elementary. It was generally safe. It was made up of two platforms that were only a few feet off the ground, a round black swing held by a chain covered in vinyl (to protect hands), and a shiny green metal track that the swing slid easily along for over twenty yards. He'd seen a couple of kids fall off it, but they always bounced back up with a smile.

As Cam climbed onto the platform, his classmates lined up on both sides of the zip line's path. Hundreds of years ago, this might have been referred to as *running the gauntlet,* a form of punishment where people found guilty of crimes would walk through two rows of soldiers who would strike them with sticks, whips, or worse!

In Cam's case, it was simply referred to as . . .

"So much fun!" Abby said as she walked among the kids, making sure they all had balls to throw. She and Gabe weren't going to throw any balls. They needed to observe the proceedings to determine if there needed to be any adjustments.

Gabe was standing alongside Cam on the platform and patting him on the back for encouragement. "You got this, buddy," he said.

Cam pulled the swing up to his body and tucked it between his legs. "We aren't gonna get in trouble for this, are we?"

Gabe shook his head and said, "The recess monitors are as excited about this as everyone else."

In the distance, their gym teacher, Mr. Largo, put a thumb up and called out, "You can do it, Cam!"

It was all the encouragement he needed. "Okay, let's do it," Cam said.

"Consider this a dry run for now," Gabe said as he climbed down and gave Cam plenty of room. "Remember, in the future you'll need to carry baked goods."

"One thing at a time," Cam said, bracing himself. "Here goes."

Then he took a few steps, leaped forward, and—*zzzz*—he was off!

The first foam balls whizzed by his body and face. Near misses.

"Wahoo!" he howled.

But as he went farther, he wouldn't be so lucky.

Pff. Plup. Pff.

Foam balls hit his shoulders. His legs. His hips. But they didn't hurt or slow him down one bit.

"You gotta do better than that!" he cried.

He probably shouldn't have said that, because they did do better.

A ball, which for some reason looked like it had holes in it, hit him in the cheek, surprising him more than hurting him.

But then a white ball that looked like a baseball hit his hand and the chain of the swing. It hurt! A lot! And it spun the swing around.

How is that possible? These things are just harmless foam, right?

Those questions were answered by the next ball, which looked like a tennis ball and screamed right toward Cam and struck him right on the throat.

"Gahhh!"

There was no other way to put it. Because it knocked the air out of him.

"Got him!" a voice yelled.

Cam reached to grab his throat with both hands, which caused him to lose his grip on the swing. More soft foam balls bounced off him until a different ball—a pure white ball—struck him in the ribs. It felt hard and rubbery.

Not like foam at all. This was the final straw. He fell with a thud to the ground. The swing spun around for a moment and then zipped along to the end of its run without him.

There were gasps. Then a hushed silence. Then Gabe and Abby rushed to Cam's side.

"Are you okay?" they both asked.

Cam coughed and sat up. "I . . . I . . . think so."

He took a breath and rubbed his eyes. His vision was blurred for a moment, but when it cleared up, he saw something that he wasn't going to forget anytime soon.

All the other kids were still standing alongside the zip line with worried looks on their faces. All except for the Penderton triplets. Those three boys were huddled together, whispering to one another.

"Nobody move!" Gabe yelled. "We need to secure the scene. A crime has been committed!"

Gabe's voice was louder and more assertive than it had ever been, and it seemed to catch everyone off guard. It also seemed to work. Nobody in the vicinity moved.

"This isn't foam," Abby said, holding up something greenish yellow. "This is a real tennis ball."

The crowd looked confused.

Gabe held up something white as he said, "And this is a real baseball."

The crowd gasped.

"The buckets have been compromised!" Gabe yelled.

"Everybody collect the evidence and bring it to us," Abby instructed.

"The evidence?" Noah asked.

"The balls!" Gabe shouted.

It started slowly, with a few kids picking up the balls and using the bottoms of their shirts like baskets to carry them.

But before long nearly everyon joined the effort, and soon there was a sea of balls collected under the zip line.

The Prime Detectives sifted through them, counting them and dividing them into groups: one group with foam balls, and the other group with balls that weren't foam.

"This is what we have," Gabe said.

Then Cam announced the count. "Nine tennis balls, seven baseballs, six lacrosse balls, three pickleballs . . . and one hundred twenty-five foam balls."

"For a total of one hundred fifty balls," Abby said.

"Interesting," Cam said, and he picked up each type of ball and felt them in his hand. They were all around the same size, but obviously the foam balls were the softest.

"They were all supposed to be foam balls, right?" Cam asked.

"That's right," Gabe said. "And there were supposed to be a total of one hundred sixty-eight of them. We're still eighteen short!"

"Do you think someone switched a few at the last minute?" Abby asked.

"It's too early to say," Gabe told her. "First we have to do some investigating."

The Prime Detectives filled the three buckets with the balls and carried them across the playground to a door that led to the gym.

Their classmates followed. Because obviously, they were curious. They were also witnesses.

"Right before recess, Mr. Largo brought the three buckets of balls from the gym and left them next to this door," Gabe said. "The buckets were then carried directly from this door across the playground to the zip line. Sanjeev, Maisie, and Kiko each carried a bucket. And why did you do that, Maisie?"

"Um . . . because you asked us to," Maisie said.

"Exactly," Gabe said. "And did anyone take the buckets from you at any point, Sanjeev?"

"No one touched my bucket," Sanjeev said.

"How about yours, Kiko?" Gabe asked.

"No one even got within ten feet of my bucket," Kiko said.

"I figured as much," Gabe said. "I have a lot of trust in the three of you. But I haven't ruled you out as suspects yet."

Sanjeev and Kiko flinched at the suggestion, but Maisie said, "It's fun to throw foam balls at people, but why would we want to hurt Cam with something harder?"

"That's the question, right?" Gabe said. "Why would anyone want to hurt Cam?"

"Indeed," Cam said. "I'm delightful."

"Let's not go overboard," Gabe said. "But let's figure out something else. Who threw the balls that knocked you down?"

"It wasn't me," Sanjeev said. "I have terrible aim."

"I know. Most kids do. Except for . . ." Then Gabe pointed two fingers at two kids and said, "Emmett and Luciana."

Emmett's face went red, and Luciana hung her head.

"Emmett is the best pitcher in Little League, and Luciana is a disc golf phenom," Gabe went on. "Their aim is amazing."

Then Emmett placed his hands over his face and cried, "It's true. I hit him with at least five balls, including the one that knocked him over. I was throwing so fast that I didn't notice they weren't all foam."

"Me too," Luciana said through tears. "I threw the one that hit his throat, but I thought the balls were all foam!"

"I believe both of you," Gabe said.

"I think we're missing something, then," Abby said. "If no one tampered with the balls, and the kids who threw the balls aren't to blame, then what happened?"

"Maybe I should go back to the beginning," Gabe said.

"Probably a good idea," Cam said.

"It started on a warm spring day over nine years ago," Gabe said. "My father drove my mother to the hospital where she was about to give birth to—"

"Jeez, not that far back," Abby said.

Gabe smiled slyly. He almost never let on when he was being sarcastic or telling a joke, but Abby could always tell. Because friends can always tell.

"Fine," he said. "Let's go back to yesterday afternoon. Abby and I were at the playground figuring out the obstacle course for Cam's training, and we saw Mr. Largo bringing foam balls into the gym through this door."

"These balls," Abby said, holding one up.

"Exactly," Gabe said. "And you remembered that on *Triumph or Caketastrophe* there's a section of their obstacle course where they shoot cupcakes at the contestants. So, I had the brilliant idea of using the foam balls to recreate that. I ran over to Mr. Largo and told him the idea, and he loved it. He said he'd have buckets of balls ready for me at recess."

Mr. Largo was standing at the back of the crowd, and he spoke up. "It seemed harmless enough. We play games where we hit each other with these foam balls all the time. And I want Cam to win on that show as much as anyone."

"That's true," Gabe said. "It's also true that there are seventeen kids in our class. Since I knew Cam would be on the zip line, and Abby and I would be watching, that means fourteen of you were going to be throwing balls. I figured we'd need around one hundred sixty-eight balls if we wanted to hit him enough to make it realistic."

"How'd you figure that?" Sanjeev asked.

"Simple," Gabe said. "I've analyzed everyone's throwing abilities in gym class over the years, and even accounting for some improvement over the summer, I knew that most of you would probably have a hit rate of around 8 percent."

Gabe was confronted with blank stares.

"What do you mean by a hit rate of 8 percent?" Kiko asked.

"I guess we haven't gotten to percentages yet in class," Gabe said. "So, I'll explain it with fractions. I mean that if you were throwing twelve balls, then you might hit your target one out of twelve times. That's on average. Maybe one of you would be unlucky and miss all your throws. But then another of you might be lucky and hit two out of twelve throws. But it all averages out to one in twelve by the end."

Not all the kids understood, but some of them now nodded, including Luciana.

"I bet my hit rate is closer to 50 percent," she said. "That's one out of two, right?"

"It is," Gabe replied. "And you're right. Your hit rate is that high. The same is true for Emmett. It was all calculated in. And I figured if every kid had twelve balls each, twelve of you would hit Cam with an average of one ball, while Luciana and Emmett would hit him with an average of six balls each. That means Cam would be hit by—"

"Twenty-four balls total," Abby said. "Which is also about one out of every seven balls."

"Right," Gabe said. "Let me show everyone how we figured that out."

Then Gabe used a stick to scratch out some equations in the dirt.

EVIDENCE

$$168 \div 14 = 12$$
BALLS KIDS

➡ 12 BALLS
per kid

"Everyone get that part?" Gabe asked. "My original plan was to divide one hundred sixty-eight balls evenly between fourteen kids. That gives us twelve balls per kid."

Most everyone nodded. It was a simple enough equation, after all.

"Great," Gabe said. "Now let's look at the twelve kids with hit rates of one out of twelve."

"How about that?" Gabe asked. "Is that clear?"

Now only some kids nodded. Others shrugged.

Cam waved his hand like he was in class. "I think it's clear that I got hit by at least twelve balls," he said with a sigh.

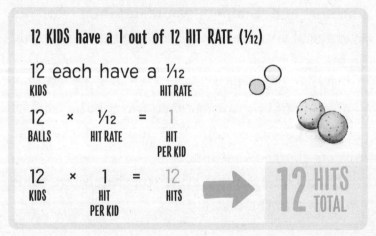

12 KIDS have a 1 out of 12 HIT RATE (¹⁄₁₂)

12 each have a ¹⁄₁₂
KIDS   HIT RATE

12   ×   ¹⁄₁₂   =   1
BALLS   HIT RATE   HIT
                         PER KID

12   ×   1   =   12   ➜   12 HITS
KIDS   HIT   HITS   TOTAL
           PER KID

"More like twice as many," Gabe said. "Because I haven't shown you the calculations for Emmett and Luciana yet. Have a look."

And Gabe scratched out some more equations.

2 KIDS (Emmett and Luciana)
have a 1 out of 2 HIT RATE (½)

2 each have a ½
KIDS   HIT RATE

12   ×   ½   =   6
BALLS   HIT RATE   HITS
                     PER KID

2   ×   6   =   12
KIDS   HITS   HITS
        PER KID

➡ 12 HITS TOTAL

"So, twenty-four hits total for all fourteen kids?" Cam asked.

"Yep," Gabe said as he scratched out more equations. "And knowing that, we can calculate the combined hit rate for everyone. First we add up all the hits . . ."

12   +   12   =   24
HITS   HITS   BALLS
(EMMETT AND LUCIANA)   (EVERYONE ELSE)   HITTING CAM

"Then we divide the total number of balls by the total number of hits to get the combined hit rate."

What is the combined hit rate for all?

$$168 \div 24 = 7$$

BALLS   BALLS
HITTING CAM

➡️ **1 OUT OF 7**
The combined hit
rate for everyone

"But there weren't one hundred sixty-eight balls," Cam said, pointing to the collection in front of them. "We found one hundred fifty for some reason."

"You're right," Gabe said. "But the hit rate would stay essentially the same. That's the thing about statistics. Fluctuations happen with small numbers, but when bigger numbers are involved, things tend to stay consistent."

"So, it'll stay one out of seven, no matter how many balls are thrown?" Cam asked.

"Or until someone either improves or gets too tired to throw anymore," Gabe said. "But let's shift our focus to the material of the balls themselves. As you said, we only found one hundred fifty balls. And even though most were foam, there were also nine tennis balls, seven baseballs, six lacrosse balls, and three pickleballs. That means the number of balls that weren't foam balls in the mix were—"

"Twenty-five balls," Abby said. "Or one out of every six balls."

$$9 + 7 + 6 + 3 = 25$$

| TENNIS BALLS | BASE-BALLS | LACROSSE BALLS | PICKLE-BALLS | NONFOAM BALLS |

"Exactly," Gabe said, writing out more equations. "And we can divide the total number of balls by the nonfoam ones to figure out what fraction of the balls were nonfoam."

$$150 \div 25 = 6$$

| TOTAL BALLS | NONFOAM BALLS |

➡ **1 OUT OF 6**
BALLS WERE NONFOAM

"I'm confused," Maisie said. "You first wrote down one out of seven. Then you wrote down one out of six. Those fractions seem really close together. Does that mean that most of the nonfoam balls hit Cam? Because I thought he was hit by mostly foam balls."

"He was," Gabe said. "Remember that the hit rate was one out of seven balls. But only one out of six of those hits came from nonfoam balls. So, the number of nonfoam balls that hit Cam was one out of every forty-two balls thrown.

You get that by multiplying the two fractions."

Gabe filled the dirt with more scribbles.

$$\frac{1}{7} \times \frac{1}{6} = \frac{1}{42}$$

HIT RATE   BALLS THAT   BALLS THROWN WERE
ARE NONFOAM   NONFOAM AND HIT CAM

➡ **1 OUT OF 42** BALLS THROWN WERE NONFOAM AND HIT CAM

"Which means between three and four nonfoam balls were thrown on target," Abby said.

"How did you figure that out?" Maisie asked.

Gabe scribbled some more and said, "She got that by multiplying all one hundred fifty balls by the fraction one out of forty-two. Which is another way of saying she divided one hundred fifty by forty-two."

$$150 \div 42 = {}^{150}\!/_{42} = \text{approximately } 3\tfrac{1}{2} \text{ (OR 3 TO 4)}$$

NONFOAM BALLS HIT THEIR TARGET

"Luciana and Emmett each threw a nonfoam ball that hit me," Cam said. "Which makes total sense because half of the hits should have been coming from them."

Gabe pumped a fist in celebration because Cam was exactly right, and he wrote out the conclusion. "So, by our calculations, you'll see that the following is true."

SOLVED **This is exactly what happened!**

3 TO 4 NONFOAM BALLS SHOULD HAVE HIT CAM

½ OF 3 TO 4 = 1½ TO 2

NONFOAM BALLS HITTING CAM   BALLS THROWN BY EMMETT AND LUCIANA

4 NONFOAM BALLS HIT CAM AND
2 WERE THROWN BY EMMETT AND LUCIANA.

The dirt was an absolute mess of equations and writing, and Gabe stood next to it all, hands proudly on his hips. The group was silent for a moment, taking time to decipher the overwhelming quantity of information, until Cam finally spoke again.

"It's all interesting, but a bit complicated, don't you think?" he said. "And I'm not sure it tells us anything."

"It tells us that the nonfoam balls were randomly scattered through the buckets and the kids," Gabe said. "None of the throwers were doing this on purpose. We can't blame them any more than we can blame clouds for dropping rain on our heads. It was bound to happen no matter what."

"I see that," Cam said. "But it doesn't explain why the other balls were in the buckets in the first place. Who could've put them in there?"

All heads turned toward the gym teacher, Mr. Largo. He was the one who filled the buckets with the balls, after all.

He held up his hands and said, "I would never endanger a student like that."

"I asked you to fill three buckets with fifty-six balls each for a total of one hundred sixty-eight balls," Gabe said. "You did that, right?"

This is when Mr. Largo's face went red, and he hung his head. "I might've had a little help."

"Who helped you?" Cam asked.

"I don't want to accuse anyone of anything," Mr. Largo said. "But those nice new triplets, Jason, Mason, and Grayson, asked if they could help fill the buckets. So, I let them."

This time the gasps from the crowd were louder than ever. And when everyone looked around, the Pendertons were nowhere to be seen.

Chapter 6

THE USUAL SUSPECTS

The hunt for the triplets was on. Kids scoured the playground, looking in secret hiding places.

No luck.

It soon became clear that they were inside the school. *But where?*

While the other students searched for the Pendertons, the Prime Detectives accompanied Mr. Largo to the gym. They wanted to understand exactly what happened with the balls, but they only had a few minutes to investigate before they had to return to class.

"While everyone was headed to lunch, I gave the triplets a tour of the gym," Mr. Largo explained as he led them across the basketball court and toward the equipment closet. "I was finishing up the tour when I remembered that I needed to collect those balls for you. There was, however, a problem. My next class was starting, and I didn't have time. So, the triplets volunteered to do it for me. They were so friendly about it, too."

"They're friendly guys," Abby said.

"Or at least they pretend to be," Cam said.

While Cam had believed that the triplets were innocent of poisoning the cookies, he was starting to doubt his instincts about them being entirely innocent. *Why else would they have put those other balls in there?*

When they finally reached the equipment closet, Abby asked, "How long did it take them to count the balls?"

"Not very long," Mr. Largo said as he turned the door handle. "I saw them leaving for lunch a few minutes later, and the balls were in the buckets right out here."

The closet was dark when Mr. Largo opened the door, so he reached in to turn on the light.

Click went the light switch. But the light didn't come on.

"That's strange," Mr. Largo said, then he reached down into his pocket and pulled out a ring of keys. There was a tiny LED flashlight on his key chain. He turned it on and shined it into the closet.

"That's even stranger," Gabe said.

Because the closet was an absolute mess. Bags of jerseys, stacks of helmets, and other equipment sat on two shelves that were mounted high up on the walls. But a third shelf had been knocked down, and a variety of balls and overturned cardboard boxes now covered the floor. There was a digital scale in the corner. And there was a small pile of broken glass.

"I think there was something more than collecting foam balls going on in here," Cam said.

Gabe stepped forward, picked up a foam ball, and placed it on the scale. The digital display lit up green and showed the weight of the ball:

2 OUNCES

"Interesting," Gabe whispered as he collected baseballs, lacrosse balls, and other balls to weigh.

When the Prime Detectives arrived back in Mrs. E.'s classroom for science class, they noticed the Penderton triplets were there. They also noticed Mrs. E. was in the corner chatting with the custodian, Mrs. Vernon.

Cam assumed she was probably asking Mrs. Vernon about the missing iPad. Which was smart. Mrs. Vernon knew the school inside and out. Their chat seemed to be a happy one, though.

They were chuckling, and Mrs. Vernon was doing something strange with her hands, curling her forefingers and thumbs and holding them over her eyes like she was pretending she was wearing a mask. Cam didn't know what that meant, but he wondered if maybe the mystery of the missing iPad had been solved.

Since Mrs. E. was distracted, she obviously didn't notice what was happening on the other side of the classroom. Kids were surrounding, and interrogating, the Penderton triplets.

"Confess," Luciana said to them with a sneer.

"We know you did it," Sanjeev added.

Maisie simply wagged a finger at them.

The Pendertons looked terrified, and once Mrs. Vernon left the room, Mrs. E. finally noticed. She came to their rescue.

"Back away," she said. "I'm sure this is another misunderstanding. But even if it isn't, this is not how we treat our classmates."

"It is when they try to hurt one of us," Kiko said.

Cam was touched by the support, but he didn't want anyone else to get hurt, so he said, "Mrs. E. is right. We don't treat our classmates like this, no matter what they may or may not have done."

This worked. The kids backed off, but the triplets still felt the need to defend themselves.

"We didn't do anything wrong," Grayson said.

"We were only trying to help," Jason said.

"We would never want to hurt anyone," Mason said.

They sounded genuine, but Cam suspected it couldn't be a coincidence that they had sabotaged the buckets of balls shortly after he had revealed their cookie screwup. This seemed an awful lot like a revenge plot. Or maybe something worse? Which made him wonder if the Pendertons were also responsible for another mystery.

"Any sign of your missing iPad, Mrs. E.?" he asked. "Did Mrs. Vernon find it for you?"

She shook her head slowly. "It's very strange, isn't it? Not a sign of it anywhere."

"I bet if someone returned it to you, then they'd be considered heroes," Cam said, and he looked at the Pendertons. They shrugged. They were either clueless as to what he was implying, or they were pretending to be clueless. He suspected the latter.

"I'm sure it'll turn up," Mrs. E. said. "But that's not my concern right now. Nor is the unfortunate accident on the playground. Right now, my concern is . . . drumroll, please . . ."

Most of the class didn't know this was a cue for them to start drumming their fingers on their desks. At least not until Maisie, who was an actual drummer, started doing it. Then one by one they joined in until the entire classroom was echoing with the sounds of finger drumsticks.

The suspense had built enough that Mrs. E. could finally shout out, "Birds!"

And a bird flew out of her sleeve.

A living, breathing bird!

It fluttered through the room, its green, yellow, and black wings catching the light.

"Whoa, is that a parrot?" Emmett asked.

That's when the bird landed on Mrs. E.'s shoulder, and she said, "A parakeet. Also known as a budgerigar, or budgie for short. His name is Mr. Mortimer Sunshine."

"Hello, Mr. Mortimer Sunshine!" a few of the kids said at the same time.

"Did your sleeve give birth to that bird?" Mason asked. "Or was that sorcery?"

"It's quite clearly a trick," Gabe said. "Sleight of hand. She snuck the bird into her sleeve when we weren't looking and then released it. Even amateur magicians can do that one."

"Gabe is correct," Mrs. E. said. "It was sleight of hand. That means that I distracted my audience and moved my hand in such a way that you wouldn't be able to see me slip the bird into my sleeve."

"I saw it," Abby admitted. "But I didn't want to ruin the trick."

"Which brings us to another thing Gabe was correct about," Mrs. E. said. "I am still an amateur. But I'm learning."

Abby noticed that the window was still open and remembered how that little black-feathered bird flew out in the morning. She didn't want Mr. Mortimer Sunshine to do the same thing, so she hurried over to it.

Beneath the window, there was a counter that ran all the way over to Mrs. E.'s desk. It was cluttered with books that were stacked higher than the window frame, so Abby pushed them aside. Then, as she was closing the window, she noticed something odd on the ground. There was a patch of dried mud with three rectangular indentations in it.

Hmm, she said to herself as she filed the image away in her Memory Palace. Then she returned to her seat.

Meanwhile, Mr. Mortimer Sunshine was making a little sound that wasn't quite a chirp and wasn't quite a screech but lived somewhere in between. Mrs. E. reached in her pocket and pulled out a little cookie made of birdseed and held it up. Mr. Mortimer Sunshine started to nibble on it.

Cam resisted the urge to say that the birdseed cookie probably tasted better than the Pendertons' cookies. But he did ask, "Why'd you bring the budgie to class?"

"Because I love animals," Mrs. E. said. "I love talking about animals. I love teaching about animals. I'd be willing to bet that I also have more pets than anyone in this room."

"We have a guinea pig and a hermit crab," Maisie announced.

"I have two dogs," Noah told everyone.

"I have three cats," Abby said proudly.

"And I have four dogs, six cats, five chickens, two goats, one rabbit, one iguana, eight hamsters, three snakes, two ferrets, and one budgie named Mr. Mortimer Sunshine," Mrs. E. said.

"How many pets in total is that, Abby?" Cam asked.

"Too many," she said, even though she knew the answer was thirty-three.

"It's the exact right amount for us," Mrs. E. said. "And I'll bring other pets to class to say hello throughout the year. But today, let's talk about birds."

Mrs. E. talked about birds. She talked about how they have hollow bones, which help them fly. Not because the hollow bones make them lighter, but because they help them breathe more efficiently. She talked about gizzards, which are part of birds' digestive systems.

The gizzards are full of stones known as gastroliths that help break down food because birds don't have teeth for chewing. And she talked about how birds evolved from dinosaurs, and so hummingbirds share a similar ancestor with T. rexes, which impressed nearly everyone in the class.

When she started talking about *Pelagornis sandersi*, which was a bird that went extinct millions of years ago, Gabe was starting to figure something out.

"*Pelagornis sandersi* had a wingspan that was over twenty feet long, which is the size of a small bus!" Mrs. E. said. "And they weighed up to ninety pounds."

"That's more than me!" Cam said. And Cam wasn't small.

Gabe jotted down some equations on a piece of paper. He slid them over to Abby, who glanced at them, nodded, and slid them back.

"A budgie weighs around an ounce," Mrs. E. said, pointing to Mr. Mortimer Sunshine. "*Pelagornis sandersi* was over one thousand times heavier!"

"And a baseball is two and a half times heavier than a foam ball," Gabe said.

The class was silent for a moment. No one knew what to say to that. So, Mrs. E. said, "That's interesting, Gabe, but what does it have to do with birds?"

"Well, firstly, both fly," Gabe said. "And I bet if a *Pelagornis sandersi* hit Cam while he was on the zip line, it would knock him off, too. A budgie? Probably not."

"We didn't do anything wrong!" the Pendertons cried.

"Not on purpose," Gabe said. "But you made a mistake again, didn't you?"

The Pendertons didn't answer, but Mrs. E. did. "Let's slow down with the accusations."

"I'm not accusing them," Gabe said. "I'm saving them."

"Saving us?" Mason said.

Gabe nodded and said, "Yes, once again." Then he held up his sheet of paper with the equations on it. "And here's the proof. I weighed different balls in the equipment closet, and I compared the weights to what we found on the playground. I wrote some equations down. Can we project them on the whiteboard?"

"Will it stop all the squabbling?" Mrs. E. asked as she grabbed the paper.

"It will," Gabe said. "Or at least I think it will. If you can't trust the math, then you can't trust anything in this world. And I feel bad for you."

In a few moments, Gabe's paper was projected on the board. It looked like this:

CONVERSION CHART
WEIGHT OF THE BALLS

1 OUNCE = PICKLEBALL

2 OUNCES = TENNIS BALL or FOAM BALL

5 OUNCES = BASEBALL or LACROSSE BALL

"I don't understand how any of that makes anyone innocent of anything," Emmet said.

The rest of the class agreed by nodding and saying, "Yeah" or "Yep" or "Mm-hmm."

"That's understandable," Gabe said. "But you'll get it once I tell you what happened. The triplets can correct me if I'm wrong."

"As long as you say we're innocent, then you're right," Jason said.

"I won't just say it, I'll prove it," Gabe told them. "Here's what happened. I asked Mr. Largo to collect one hundred sixty-eight foam balls for me and to put them in three buckets of fifty-six foam balls each. Since I knew everyone's throwing accuracy, I calculated that around twenty-four balls would hit Cam, which would be good practice for when he was on *Triumph or Caketastrophe* getting pelted with cupcakes."

"As you already told everyone," Cam said.

"Mr. Largo didn't have time to count out the balls," Gabe went on. "So, he asked the Penderton triplets to do it for him."

"As *he* already told everyone," Abby said.

"Yes, but everyone didn't see what was in the equipment closet," Gabe said. "Cam and Abby, do you remember what was in there?"

"Well, it was a big mess, with a bunch of boxes and balls on the floor," Cam told the class.

"Plus, some broken glass and a broken shelf,"

Abby said.

"Oh, and it was really dark, and the light didn't work," Cam said. "Which surprised Mr. Largo."

"Plus, there was a scale for weighing things," Abby said.

"All important pieces of our story," Gabe said. "You see, the Penderton triplets wanted to count out the balls for Mr. Largo, but they ran into a little problem. The balls were all kept in cardboard boxes on the shelf in the closet. The shelf was too high for the triplets to reach, so they tried to pull themselves up to it, which caused the shelf to fall, which scattered a variety of balls throughout the room and broke the lightbulb. Am I right, Pendertons?"

The Pendertons simply stared in surprise and nodded.

"But that's not all," Gabe went on. "Now that they had a bunch of balls on the floor and no light to see them, did the triplets simply roll them out into the gym and count them? Nope. They just took the three buckets and scooped balls up. Then they weighed the buckets on the scale they found in the closet and added or removed balls until each bucket weighed exactly seven pounds. They were clever enough to weigh a foam ball first. The foam balls weighed two ounces each. So, they could calculate that fifty-six foam balls weighed one hundred twelve ounces, or seven pounds. They were also clever enough to subtract the weight of each bucket from their calculations when they put them on the scale. But they were not observant enough to realize that there weren't only foam balls in the buckets. There were other balls with different weights mixed in."

"It was Jason's idea," Mason said, pointing to his brother.

"And it was a brilliant idea," Jason said. "It was much faster than counting and much easier to do in the dark."

"Plus, he told us to do it," Grayson said, pointing at Cam.

Cam was shocked. He put a hand on his chest. "*Moi?*" he said (which is French for *me*, as any good chef knows).

"You told us it was always better to weigh ingredients, so that's what we did!" Grayson said.

"Not exactly what I meant," Cam said. "I don't know of any recipes that call for baseballs."

Mrs. E. pointed to Gabe's equations on the whiteboard. "Can everyone follow what happened?" she asked.

"Um . . . kinda?" Luciana said.

EVIDENCE

What we asked Mr. Largo to get us:

168 FOAM BALLS

16 OUNCES = **1** POUND

168 FOAM BALLS × 2 OUNCES = 336 OUNCES TOTAL

336 OUNCES ÷ 16 OUNCES PER POUND = 21 POUNDS

And 168 foam balls weighing 21 pounds split into 3 buckets is . . .

168 FOAM BALLS ÷ 3 BUCKETS = 56 FOAM BALLS PER BUCKET

21 POUNDS ÷ 3 BUCKETS = 7 POUNDS PER BUCKET

➡️ So, we should have had 56 foam balls in each bucket weighing **7 POUNDS PER BUCKET**

What we actually found at the scene of the crime:

150 BALLS

A Mix of:
- 125 Foam Balls
- 9 Tennis Balls
- 7 Baseballs
- 6 Lacrosse Balls
- 3 Pickleballs

125 FOAM BALLS × 2 OUNCES = TOTAL WEIGHT of 250 OUNCES

9 TENNIS BALLS × 2 OUNCES = TOTAL WEIGHT of 18 OUNCES

7 BASEBALLS × 5 OUNCES = TOTAL WEIGHT of 35 OUNCES

6 LACROSSE BALLS × 5 OUNCES = TOTAL WEIGHT of 30 OUNCES

3 PICKLEBALLS × 1 OUNCE = TOTAL WEIGHT of 3 OUNCES

GRAND TOTAL WEIGHT

250 + 18 + 35 + 30 + 3 = 336 OUNCES

336 OUNCES ÷ 16 OUNCES PER POUND = 21 POUNDS

21 POUNDS ÷ 3 BUCKETS = 7 POUNDS PER BUCKET

7 POUNDS PER BUCKET That's the exact same weight as what we expected Mr. Largo to give us!

Here's one way you could split those balls up into 3 buckets that weigh 7 pounds each:

BUCKET #1

42 FOAM BALLS = 84 OUNCES
3 TENNIS BALLS = 6 OUNCES
2 BASEBALLS = 10 OUNCES
2 LACROSSE BALLS = 10 OUNCES
2 PICKLEBALLS = 2 OUNCES

84+6+10+10+2 = 112 OUNCES

BUCKET #2

41 FOAM BALLS = 82 OUNCES
2 TENNIS BALLS = 4 OUNCES
3 BASEBALLS = 15 OUNCES
2 LACROSSE BALLS = 10 OUNCES
1 PICKLEBALL = 1 OUNCE

82+4+15+10+1 = 112 OUNCES

BUCKET #3

42 FOAM BALLS = 84 OUNCES
4 TENNIS BALLS = 8 OUNCES
2 BASEBALLS = 10 OUNCES
2 LACROSSE BALLS = 10 OUNCES

84+8+10+10 = 112 OUNCES

Each bucket weighs 112 ounces, which is 7 pounds.

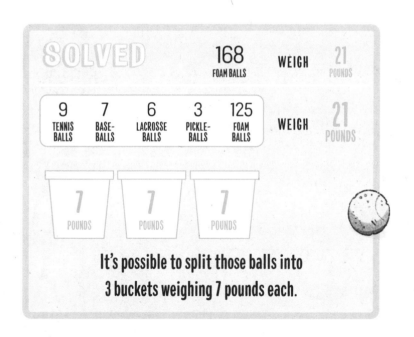

SOLVED

168 FOAM BALLS   WEIGH   21 POUNDS

9	7	6	3	125
TENNIS BALLS	BASE-BALLS	LACROSSE BALLS	PICKLE-BALLS	FOAM BALLS

WEIGH   21 POUNDS

7 POUNDS   7 POUNDS   7 POUNDS

It's possible to split those balls into
3 buckets weighing 7 pounds each.

THEREFORE . . . THE PENDERTONS ARE INNOCENT!

"It's simple," Gabe said. "Instead of counting out the foam balls, the Pendertons scooped up random balls in the dark. Some balls, such as baseballs and lacrosse balls, weighed more than foam balls. Some balls, such as pickleballs, weighed less. Some balls, such as tennis balls, weighed the same. Which means they ended up with three buckets containing seven pounds of balls each, but some of those balls were not the type of balls we should've been throwing at Cam. And that's what caused him to crash.

The moral of the story is this: Don't take shortcuts."

"Actually," Mrs. E. said, "I think there's a better moral."

"Which is?" Gabe asked.

"It's probably best not to throw *any* balls at our classmates, even if they're training for a cooking competition and obstacle course show. At least not during school hours."

It was a good point.

Chapter 7

RETURN TO THE MEMORY PALACE

The Prime Detectives had solved yet another mystery, and the Penderton triplets were off the hook once again. But there was still tension in the air. It was only the first day, and things kept going wrong. Not to mention the fact that Mrs. E.'s iPad was still missing!

"Do you think she's just forgetful?" Gabe asked as he, Cam, and Abby walked to art class. "Maybe she misplaced it and doesn't remember where."

"She had never met any of us before, but she remembered things about everyone in class," Cam said. "Plus, she taught us about the Memory Palace. It seems like she has an excellent memory."

"Good point," Abby said. "What do you think about the window?"

"What window?" Gabe said.

"In Mrs. E.'s room. It was open. And when I looked outside, I saw some weird indentations in the dried mud below it," Abby said.

"Like footprints?" Cam asked.

Abby shook her head. "Not unless it's some sort of three-legged robot."

"What are you saying?" Gabe asked.

"Do you think someone climbed in through the window and stole the iPad?" Abby asked.

The two boys thought it over for a moment.

"It's definitely possible," Gabe said, and Cam nodded in agreement.

"I'd like to investigate more," Abby said. "Do you think I can convince Miss Pelican to hold art class outside today?"

Cam smiled and said, "Everyone knows that Abby the Abacus can convince almost anyone to do almost anything."

Cam was right. Abby could be quite persuasive. In fact, in third grade, she had persuaded their teacher, Mr. Fritz, to cancel classes for the day and let them watch movies instead.

It's true.

It was a Friday morning when she explained to Mr. Fritz that, in the years since they started kindergarten, the third graders had received at least six more hours of schooling than any other grade.

This didn't seem to make sense at first. That is, until Abby explained that due to shuffling classroom locations throughout the years, she and her fellow third graders had the shortest walks between classes, which meant they were in their classrooms for at least thirty seconds more per day than any other grade. If you added all that extra time up over four years, it was more than six hours of extra schooling. Abby could do these calculations in her head, but she had Gabe prepare a small booklet with a breakdown of the equations, as well as maps of the school, detailing the routes to classes. She handed that booklet to Mr. Fritz.

"We'd like to even things out by watching movies today," Abby said.

Mr. Fritz reviewed the booklet, scratching his chin and saying *hmm* to himself over and over again. Finally, when he reached the end, he sighed and said, "Okay. What do you want to watch?"

The other third graders cheered.

Abby and her friends were now fourth graders, and they didn't have any extra time on their hands. Plus, their art teacher, Miss Pelican, was impervious to math equations. In other words, she didn't care about them and what they proved or didn't prove. So, Abby needed a different way to convince her teacher to hold class outside. She tried to be clever.

"Vitamin D is perhaps the most essential vitamin," Abby told Miss Pelican at the beginning of class. "And did you know that you get it from sunshine?"

"I did know that, but this was a good reminder," Miss Pelican said, not getting the hint.

Abby tried again. "The clouds are quite stunning today, Miss Pelican," she said. "It would be fun to paint them."

"It would indeed. I always enjoy painting clouds," Miss Pelican said. But she left it at that.

Clearly, Miss Pelican wasn't getting the

message, so Abby tried some even stronger persuasion. "A recent study found that children who create art using things found in nature have more empathy, creativity, and ultimately get into better colleges than their peers," Abby told her teacher.

"I read that study," Gabe said, trying to help the cause. "It was quite convincing."

"Interesting," Miss Pelican said. "And I'm impressed that fourth graders are already considering colleges. Your generation is quite forward-thinking."

Abby was frustrated, which rarely happened.

And Cam was a bit more direct, which usually happened.

"Miss Pelican," he said. "Can we have class outside today?"

"Of course!" Miss Pelican said. "I thought you'd never ask."

So, yes, Abby could be persuasive, but sometimes simply asking is better than persuading.

Five minutes later, Miss Pelican and the kids were sitting on the grass near the playground—a perfect place for Abby to start her investigation.

As the rest of the class sketched with charcoal, Abby closed her eyes. She wasn't imagining what she was going to draw, and she wasn't sleepy. She was entering her Memory Palace.

The Memory Palace was instinctual for Abby at this point. Some people had what they called a *photographic memory*, where they could see something in the past and be able to instantly bring that exact image back into their head, as though they were looking at an old photograph. Abby's memory wasn't like that. She had to use techniques such as the Memory Palace to remember things. But she used those techniques all the time. The previous day, in fact.

She and Gabe had met at the playground to plan the obstacle course for Cam. There were a variety of elements to consider—from the climbing dome to the monkey bars and zip line— and they had to be in a particular order that wasn't necessarily intuitive. For instance, rather than going from one obstacle to the next closest obstacle, Gabe had devised a complicated route that zigged and zagged and sometimes revisited the same spots multiple times.

So, Abby started building her Memory Palace, incorporating all the elements of the obstacle course. She didn't even think about doing it. It came naturally.

The tendency to slip other things into her palace came naturally, too.

These were things that Abby wasn't necessarily trying to remember but still found their way into her Memory Palace because they were nearby.

Therefore, when she was in the kitchen of her palace adding an old-fashioned scale so that she'd remember the seesaw, she also added a *broom*. When she was in the dining room of her palace adding a round chandelier so that she'd remember a tire swing, she also added a large *mirror*. And when she was in the backyard of her palace adding a twisty slide so that she'd remember . . . a twisty slide, she also added *three ants*.

So, what are those extra things that slipped in? What do the broom, mirror, and ants represent?

The *broom* represented Mrs. Vernon, the custodian who Abby had seen out of the corner of her eye. She was collecting sticks and brush for the evening's bonfire and putting them in a wheelbarrow. And propped up on the handles of the wheelbarrow, she was carrying what looked like a small dog crate.

The *mirror* represented a window to Mrs. E.'s classroom. It was the same window that the Prime Detectives had found open that morning. But on the previous day, it definitely had been closed.

Abby remembered it because she saw it from the outside. She had walked over and peeked into the classroom. She could see that no one was in the room, and since the room was dark, she could also see her faint reflection in the glass. And that's why the window was represented by a mirror.

Finally, the *three ants* represented the . . . Penderton triplets.

The Penderton triplets were there yesterday! Not at the playground, but Abby had spotted them in the distance, walking together toward the school. She didn't know who they were, of course, and they weren't close enough for her to recognize that they were identical triplets.

They looked almost as small as, well, ants. But there was something about them that had seemed different, and so they found their way into her Memory Palace, too.

Abby opened her eyes. Now she had a clearer picture of what was going on behind the school the previous day. *But is any of it connected to Mrs. E.'s missing iPad?*

It was hard to say. She needed to learn more. Abby stood up with her paper and charcoal. "Do you mind if I walk around a bit and draw a few things I see?" she asked Miss Pelican.

"Wander as you will," Miss Pelican said. "Let your muse be your guide."

"I think our muses are telling us to join her," Gabe said, grabbing Cam by the arm and pulling him up.

"Be inspired, young artists," Miss Pelican said. "Be inspired!"

Abby inspired the other two to walk over to the window to investigate. It was closed again, and they could see their faint reflections in it. There was no obvious place to hold the window frame if a person wanted to open it from the outside. They would've had to press their hands to the glass and push it up, and that's assuming it was unlocked.

"Notice any fingerprints on the glass?" Gabe asked.

"We could dust it with some flour?" Cam said.

"That'll make the fingerprints show up."

Abby took a step back in surprise. "Do you have flour with you right now?"

"Not right now," Cam said. "But I've been known to carry flour on occasion. Never know when you might need to whip up a nice béchamel sauce."

"We may not have flour, but we do have this," Gabe said, and he held up the stick of charcoal he had been using to draw.

"How will that help?" Cam asked.

"Watch," Gabe said, and he crushed a bit of the charcoal with his fingers. "Even better than flour."

Black dust fell into Gabe's open hand. Then he proceeded to blow the dust on the window. The idea was that if there were fingerprints there, then the dust would stick to them and make them show up. Then the culprit could be identified.

But the dust didn't seem to do anything. It simply hit the glass and fell to the ground.

"Oh, well," Cam said.

Gabe grumbled.

But Abby wasn't discouraged.

"We may not see any evidence of fingerprints,

but I think this is interesting," she said, and she pointed to a patch of mud below the window. The three rectangular indentations she had noticed earlier were still there. They formed a triangle.

"Weird," Gabe said. "Any footprints to go with them?"

"Perhaps three identical sets?" Cam asked.

There wasn't even one set of footprints in the mud, but that didn't mean that no one had walked by the window in the last day. The area surrounding the patch of mud was all grass, and people tended not to leave footprints in grass.

However, if someone had tried to climb in through the window when the mud was there, they would have left a mark of some kind.

"Maybe those three indentations are from a stool that someone used to climb in?" Gabe said.

"Weird stool," Abby said. "Plus, the window isn't that high off the ground. I bet most kids are tall enough that they could climb into it without a stool."

"Does that mean we should be looking for some kindergartners as suspects?" Cam said jokingly.

The others laughed, but they also knew it was

unwise to rule anyone out at this point.

Before they rejoined the rest of their classmates, Gabe took what was left of his stick of charcoal and drew three dark splotches on his piece of paper.

"What is that?" Cam asked.

Gabe pointed to the mud. "We don't have phones, so we can't take a photo. But we need crime scene pictures, don't we?"

"What do we know?" Gabe asked the other two as they walked back into the school at the end of art class.

"You and I were at the playground yesterday from 3:00 p.m. to 4:00 p.m., right?" Abby said.

"Right," Gabe said. "And so were the Penderton triplets."

"Mrs. E. said she left her iPad in her room at 3:00 p.m.," Cam said. "The window was closed when she left."

"So, the window was opened sometime between 4:00 p.m. and this morning when we arrived," Cam said.

"There were no obvious fingerprints on the

window, so I'm not convinced someone opened it from the outside," Gabe said.

"But there were those indentations in the mud," Abby said. "They weren't there yesterday before 4:00 p.m., because I walked over to the window, and I didn't see them."

"And if it was muddy already, you would've left footprints," Gabe said.

"The mud!" Cam exclaimed.

"What about it?" Gabe said.

"We need to do some research," Cam said. "To the library!"

"But we have to go to our next class," Abby said.

"Our next class is free time in the library," Gabe reminded her.

"Okay then," Abby said. "To the library!"

The librarian, Ms. Santiago, was happy to help. She was always there for the Prime Detectives when they needed assistance with research. She never laughed at their questions or questioned their theories. She sincerely enjoyed watching them figure out mysteries.

While the other kids in class browsed the books (the Pendertons, for example, were interested in trilogies), Ms. Santiago led Abby, Cam, and Gabe to a computer in the back. They sat in chairs as she hovered over them, reaching forward so she could touch the keyboard and mouse and navigate the web browser.

"We need to see the weather," Gabe told her.

Ms. Santiago pointed to the window and said, "Get up and have a look. Perfect first day of school. Clear skies. Ideal for the bonfire."

Cam smiled and said, "We don't need the weather right now."

"Right," Ms. Santiago said with a wink, then she tapped some keys. "Getting the forecast is easy enough."

"Not the forecast, either," Abby said. "We need *yesterday's* weather. Specifically, when it rained at school."

"Okay," Ms. Santiago said, tapping some more keys. "I know a database to check. We have a weather station behind the school, so the info should be quite accurate."

In seconds, she brought up a screen that showed weather data from the nearest weather station for the past few days. There was a graph showing the change in temperature, the amount of precipitation, and so on.

"Says here that it rained heavily from 4:30 p.m. to 5:30 p.m. And then it stopped, and the sun came out," Gabe said, pointing at the screen.

"That means the mud was formed sometime around then and dried after," Cam said.

Gabe nodded.

"Does that mean that whatever left the prints was moved before or after it dried?" Abby asked.

"Not 100 percent sure, but I'd guess *after* it dried," Gabe said. "Because those prints weren't smudged at all. They probably would've been if the mud was wet when the unknown object was moved."

Ms. Santiago rapped her knuckles on the desk

and then turned to walk away. "Sounds like you have another doozy of a mystery to solve. Can't wait to hear what you find."

"I can't, either!" Cam said.

It was always wise to carry hard copies of data, so Cam printed what they saw on the screen, grabbed the sheet, folded it up, and slipped it in his pocket. As he walked away from the printer, he spotted a book of baking recipes on display. He grabbed that, too, so he could take it home and study it—yet another way for him to get ready for *Triumph or Caketastrophe*!

Meanwhile, Abby pulled a birding guide off the shelf. Mrs. E.'s presentation, with the help of Mr. Mortimer Sunshine, had sparked an interest in all things avian. She'd never thought much about birds, but now she wanted to know everything there was to know about them.

At the same time, Gabe stared at his charcoal drawing of the indentations in the mud, trying to figure out what on earth might have made them. On the one hand, the Prime Detectives now had plenty of evidence and information to keep them occupied. On the other hand, they were no closer to a solution to the day's biggest mystery.

Chapter 8

THE MAGIC NUMBER

The end of the day was drawing near. Sometimes it took more than one day for the Prime Detectives to solve a mystery, but it felt wrong to leave a mystery unsolved on the first day of school. Luckily, it was time for math class.

Back in the classroom, Mrs. E. held up her abacus and said, "Let's talk numbers."

Gabe nodded in satisfaction. Cam flashed Mrs. E. a thumbs-up. And Abby pumped her fist. Forget recess. Math class was always the highlight of their day because it was the best time for problem solving.

"What sort of numbers are we talking about today?" Abby asked. "Irrational numbers? Imaginary numbers?"

"That's a bit complex for fourth grade," Mrs. E. said. "How about the number three?"

"This isn't preschool!" Maisie protested. "We already know about three!"

"Do you?" Mrs. E. asked as she moved three wooden beads across the abacus. "Do you really?"

"Sure," Maisie said. "It comes after one and two and before four. What else do you need to know?"

"A lot," Mrs. E. said. "Do you know how to figure out if a number is divisible by three?"

"De-*what*-able?" Maisie asked.

"Divisible," Mrs. E. said again. "It means if I have a number, can I figure out what whole numbers it can be divided by? For instance, the number forty is divisible by one, two, four, five, eight, ten, and twenty. Why? Because you can use those numbers in multiplication equations that result in forty. Such as . . ."

Mrs. E. wrote a series of equations on the whiteboard.

$$1 \times 40 = 40 \qquad 2 \times 2 \times 10 = 40$$
$$2 \times 20 = 40 \qquad 2 \times 4 \times 5 = 40$$
$$4 \times 10 = 40 \qquad 2 \times 2 \times 2 \times 5 = 40$$
$$5 \times 8 = 40$$

"But you were talking about three," Maisie said. "I don't see three in any of those equations."

"That's right," Mrs. E. said. "Because forty isn't divisible by three. But what are some numbers that are?"

Maisie thought for a moment, and then said, "Six?"

"Bingo!" Mrs. E. said. "Two times three equals six, so six is divisible by three."

"Thirty!" Emmett shouted.

"Indeed," Mrs. E. said. "There are ten threes in thirty, so thirty is divisible by three."

Abby said, "Four billion, five hundred sixty-nine million, nine hundred forty-one thousand, three hundred thirty-seven."

Some of the kids in the class flinched as though the number was so large that it might crush them, but Mrs. E. simply smiled, then she started moving the beads on her abacus.

"Abby is right," she said after a few moments. "That number is divisible by three. And in a few minutes, you'll all know how she figured that out. And you won't even need a tablet, a calculator, or an abacus."

"That's not possible," Maisie said. "That number is too big."

"Seems that way," Mrs. E. said. "But let's start somewhere even easier. Let's talk about *one* and *two* first."

"Sweet. Binary code," Gabe whispered to Cam, but Cam didn't know what he was talking about.

"Figuring out which numbers are divisible by one is super easy," Mrs. E. went on. "Every number in the universe is divisible by one, because every number times one equals itself. See? Easy!"

"Two is easy as well," Cam said. "Every even number in the universe is divisible by two, because every even number can be cut in half."

"Exactly right!" Mrs. E. said. "But let's get back to *three*—magical *three*!—and let's focus on a very large number. Here's Abby's number."

Mrs. E. wrote the number on the whiteboard:

4,569,941,337

"Is it divisible by one?" Mrs. E. asked the class.

"Yes!" the class answered.

"Is it divisible by two?" she asked.

"No!" the class answered.

"That's right," Mrs. E. said. "Because it ends in seven, which makes it an odd number, and only even numbers are divisible by two."

"Are all odd numbers divisible by three?" Sanjeev asked.

Gabe spoke before Mrs. E. could answer. "Only one third of them are," he told Sanjeev. "The same goes for even numbers. One out of three even numbers is divisible by three as well. That means you have a one in three chance of guessing if a number is divisible by three. That's a good batting average, but not great odds on a math test."

"I couldn't have said it better myself," Mrs. E. remarked.

"So, Abby didn't guess?" Kiko asked.

Abby shook her head.

"I told you three is a magic number," Mrs. E. said. "Because there's a trick you can learn. Watch this."

Mrs. E. went to the whiteboard and drew addition signs between the one-digit numerals that made up Abby's number.

4,569,941,337 becomes
$$4 + 5 + 6 + 9 + 9 + 4 + 1 + 3 + 3 + 7$$

"Even I can do that equation," Cam said.

"We all can," Mrs. E. said. "Follow along with me."

Then she wrote out the steps on the whiteboard.

4,569,941,337

4 + 5 = 9	37 + 1 = 38
9 + 6 = 15	38 + 3 = 41
15 + 9 = 24	41 + 3 = 44
24 + 9 = 33	44 + 7 = 51
33 + 4 = 37	

Then she put an addition sign between the five and the one, turning 51 into:

5 + 1 =

"What's the answer?" Mrs. E. asked.

"Six," everyone said.

"Is six divisible by three?" Mrs. E. asked.

"Of course," Maisie said. "I already told you it was."

"So, there you have it," Mrs. E. said.

51 turns into 5+1 = 6

➡ 6 is divisible by 3

Maisie's face scrunched up in confusion. "What exactly do we have?"

"If you add up the numerals that make up any number, no matter how long or short, and the answer is divisible by three, then that number is divisible by three," Abby said. "It also works for nine."

Mrs. E. snapped her fingers and pointed at Abby. "Right again. Let's try some other numbers."

She wrote equations on the board as she spoke.

"Is five hundred twenty-five divisible by three?" she asked.

525 $5 + 2 + 5 = 12$
$1 + 2 = 3$

525 is divisible by 3

"Yes!" the class said.

Abby did the calculation in her head and announced, "Five hundred twenty-five divided by three equals one hundred seventy-five."

"How about 4,639?" Mrs. E. asked. "Is it divisible by three?"

4,639 $4 + 6 + 3 + 9 = 22$
$2 + 2 = 4$

4,639 is not divisible by 3

"No!" the class said.

"Right," Mrs. E. said. "Because four isn't divisible by three. What about 95,706? Is it divisible by three?"

95,706 9 + 5 + 7 + 0 + 6 = 27
2 + 7 = 9

95,706 is divisible by 3

"Yes!" the class said.

"Which gets you 31,902," Abby told them.

"It works for nine, too, doesn't it?" Cam asked. "So that third number is also divisible by nine, right, Abby?"

Abby nodded. "And when you divide it by nine, you get 10,634."

"Well, it appears that nine is a magic number, too, isn't it?" Mrs. E. said.

"Fine," Maisie said. "Three and nine are magic. But why do I need to know if some big number is divisible by three?"

"If you have a gallon of chocolate milk and two brothers, you definitely need to know," Jason explained.

"We always gotta have equal amounts," Mason said.

"We wish everything in the world was divisible by three," Grayson added with a sigh.

And that's when Abby remembered something.

She reached in her pocket and pulled out the paper that had been stuck on Gabe's shoe earlier that day.

It had a dark sticky stain on it, and someone had written: 128IN3

Cam had assumed it was a license plate number, but Abby wasn't so sure.

She sniffed the paper for a moment. It smelled . . . strange. *Sweet but sour?*

Then she read the numbers and letters again.

Maybe it was supposed to be . . .

The Prime Detectives sat together on the bus home. They all lived in the same neighborhood, which helped with their investigations. They could share theories on the bus, or ride bikes to each other's houses and go through evidence.

"What do we know?" Cam asked Gabe and Abby.

"We know that Mrs. E. left her iPad in her room at 3:00 p.m. yesterday, and it was gone by 8:00 a.m. today," Gabe said.

"And we know that the door was locked at 3:00 p.m.," Abby said. "But sometime after 4:00 p.m., the window was opened."

Cam reached into his pocket and pulled out the printed page of the weather data. "According to this, it rained heavily from 4:30 p.m. to 5:30 p.m.," he said. "Do you think the window was open then?"

Abby shook her head. "There were a lot of books on the counter near the window that weren't damp, so I think it must've been opened after the rain."

"It appears the window of time for the window to be open is closing," Gabe said, and he reached into his pocket and pulled out the drawing of the three indentations in the mud. "And remember, there was something outside the window that left marks in the mud and then was removed after the mud dried."

He put his paper next to Cam's paper. "The sun was out for another hour, and it was quite warm, so the mud could've dried quickly," Cam said.

"Do you think the object could have moved by 8:00 p.m.?" Abby asked.

"Or as late as this morning," Gabe said. "You didn't notice the indentations until after lunch, right?"

Abby nodded. "Do you think whatever was there helped the person open the window from the outside? Remember, there were no fingerprints."

"I'm not sure," Gabe said as he looked at the drawing. "Do we have any other evidence?"

"I'm not sure if this is evidence," Abby said as she reached in her pocket and pulled out her piece of paper, the one with the dark sticky stain and the 128IN3 written on it. "But do you mind sniffing this?"

She pushed the paper toward Cam, and his eyes went wide. "You want me to smell some garbage?"

"I'm not sure it's garbage," Abby said. "Just sniff it and tell me what you think made that stain."

Cam shrugged—*Sure, why not?*—and he gave the paper a good sniff.

"Hmm," he said. "It's gone sour, but it's clearly something we all love."

"Which is?" Abby asked.

"Chocolate milk," Cam said.

"Interesting," Gabe said.

Chapter 9

THE TREACHEROUS TRIPLET THEOREM

Abby's parents didn't know what to do with her. Actually, that's not entirely true. They knew to keep her fed and dressed and happy and in school and all that parenting stuff. But they didn't always know how to deal with her relentless and enthusiastic love of numbers.

Abby's mom was a painter. Her dad was an English professor. They were terrible with numbers. They were always late. They messed up recipes. They made bad financial decisions. One might think they were the Pendertons' parents, rather than Abby's.

But they were definitely Abby's parents. From her freckles, the gap between her front teeth, and her long legs that came from her mom, to her dark eyes, her thick eyebrows, and her curly hair that came from her dad, Abby looked like a combination of the two. And they all had infectious laughs and optimistic outlooks on life.

Still, Abby's ability to do complex calculations and solve impossible puzzles was, quite frankly, puzzling to her mom and dad. So, they did what they could to support her. They encouraged her passion and cleared the way for her to explore it on her own. They bought her any math book she wanted and sent her to camps where she figured out mazes and escape rooms. When she excitedly told them that Gabe gave her a nickname—the Abacus—they first had to ask her what an abacus was, but then they embraced the new moniker. Whenever she accomplished something that they didn't understand, they didn't ask her to explain. They simply hugged her and kissed her forehead and told her that they were proud of her.

"How was the first day of fourth grade?" Abby's father asked, looking up from a book when she arrived home from school. "Figure out the secrets of time travel yet?"

"Not yet," Abby said, emptying her backpack on the cluttered dining room table. "But I do have a new case to solve."

"I'm intrigued," her mom said, setting down

her paintbrush and stepping out of her small studio. "Any way we can help?"

Abby showed them the stained piece of paper.

"Looks like a license plate number," her dad said.

"Nope," Abby said.

"Looks like chocolate milk was spilled on it," her mom said.

Abby pointed a finger at her mom. "Exactly. How did you know?"

"I once did a mural using only chocolate products," she said. "It looked, and tasted, great. Until the milk went sour."

"If it's not a license plate number, what is it?" her dad asked.

"I think it says 128 IN 3, so it probably means somebody was trying to figure out how to divide one hundred twenty-eight of something into three equal portions," Abby said.

"What's the answer?" her mom asked.

"You can't divide one hundred twenty-eight evenly into three equal portions,"

Abby said, "because you get forty-two and two thirds. But the person who wrote this might not have even gotten that far."

"Who wrote it?" her dad asked.

"I think it was one of the identical triplets who arrived today," Abby said. "And I think they may have stolen Mrs. E.'s iPad."

A worried look fell over her mom's face.

"Identical triplets?" her mom asked. "I pity their parents."

Her dad looked worried, too, and he said, "And you think they've stolen an iPad? That's a big accusation."

"I know," Abby said as she walked toward her bedroom with her book about birds tucked under her arm. "That's why I need to figure out more."

She flopped on her bed and got comfortable. Then she opened the book to the index at the back. She checked the index for *weight*.

Meanwhile, Cam had returned to his house, where his three elder sisters were celebrating the first day of school by choreographing a dance sequence in the front yard. Like all their dances, it was elaborate and enthusiastic, though not exactly expert.

When they saw their little brother, they turned off their music and surrounded him. Cam's eldest sister, Toni, told him, "You're gonna be our cameraman, and we're gonna go viral."

"Sorry, I've got crimes to solve!" he shouted as he pushed his way through them and headed for the house.

"Nothing in this world is as important as your flesh and blood, Cam," his middle sister, Kelly, said.

"Unless it involves you making us some of your famous french fries," his youngest sister, Raquel, added.

"I'll make everyone french fries later," Cam said as he walked through the door. "And don't worry. I'll make an equal amount for each of you."

Cam knew his sisters were always arguing about who got more or less of something, so whenever he cooked for the family, which was most days, he made sure to give the exact same portions to his sisters, even if it meant there was a little less for himself.

He suspected the same was true of the Penderton triplets. On the bus, he, Abby, and Gabe had put some things together. Cam knew by the smell that the stain on Abby's piece of paper was chocolate milk. Gabe pointed out that the

Pendertons loved chocolate milk.

And Abby figured out that the letters and numbers weren't a license plate, but instead said 128 IN 3, which probably meant the Pendertons were trying to split one hundred twenty-eight things into three equal parts.

According to Mrs. E.'s rule, that couldn't be done because one plus two plus eight equaled eleven, and one plus one equaled two. Two was not divisible by three.

But what did the triplets have one hundred twenty-eight of that they were trying to split up? Cam had the cookbook he'd taken out of the library in his hand, and he carried it to the kitchen, where he looked up something important that he was always forgetting: conversions.

Gabe had a routine when he came home after school. Water the plants. Make his bed. Unpack his backpack, then repack it for the next day of school.

As he was unpacking his backpack, he pulled out

his drawing of the three rectangles. He placed it on the coffee table and examined it.

"What's that?" a squeaky voice asked.

It was Gabe's little sister, Emma. She was in third grade. She was a good kid, a curious kid, and an annoying kid all at once. As little siblings tended to be.

"I'm not sure what it is," Gabe said. "And I doubt you know, either."

Gabe tolerated his sister for the most part, and he sometimes even asked for her help solving mysteries involving younger students at Arithmos Elementary. Some people called her friendly and persuasive, while others called her a snoop. Either way, she was very good at finding out information.

"Looks like a symbol for a secret society," she said. "Or maybe a burn mark that an alien spaceship would've left if it landed in a wheat field."

"It was found in the mud," Gabe explained.

"Doesn't rule either out," Emma said. "It's gotta be from an alien spaceship. Or a secret society. Or a secret alien spaceship society."

Gabe couldn't rule a lot of things out, but he knew he could safely rule those options out. "If you want to help, get me some scissors," he told his sister.

Emma seemed to pull the scissors out of thin air, slapping them down on the table almost immediately. "I'm always prepared," she said.

"Thanks," Gabe said, picking up the scissors and then cutting the three rectangles out of paper and placing the rectangles on the ground. "This is how it looked. Can you think of anything, besides alien spaceships, that would make these marks?"

"Let's see," Emma said, and she carried the rectangles through the house, placing them on the floor under the legs of tables, dressers, chairs, and so on. Of course, nothing matched.

Almost everything had two or four legs. If something had three legs—like a tripod or an easel—then the ends of the legs were always small and round. They would not have left rectangular marks.

"We should check outside," Gabe suggested.

They faced the same problem outside. They found some things that left rectangular marks and some things that left three marks that formed a triangle, but nothing that did both.

"Maybe there were three separate things," Emma said, "like each of those triplets standing on pieces of wood."

"Why on earth would they be doing that?"

"To be taller maybe?" Emma said with a shrug. "Don't ask me to explain triplets."

The reason Emma had mentioned wood was because they were standing in front of a pile of firewood in their yard.

Their parents ordered a cord of wood every fall that they used in their fireplace. Gabe enjoyed a good fire. However, what he didn't enjoy was moving the wood and stacking it in the woodshed, which had been his job for the last couple years.

"The woodshed!" Gabe said, suddenly realizing something.

"What about it?" Emma said.

"Follow me," he told her as he rushed across the yard with the three rectangles in his hand.

The Prime Detectives met later that afternoon at the window outside Mrs. E.'s classroom. Their parents had brought them to school to attend the evening celebration and bonfire. It was a perfect time for the three to share their theories about what happened.

"Can I start?" Cam asked.

"I don't think we could stop you from starting even if we wanted to," Gabe said.

"Fair enough," Cam said. "But it's good that I'm going first because I think I have this case cracked."

Gabe rolled his eyes. "We'll see."

But Abby said, "Tell us!"

"Okay, so yesterday the Penderton triplets were timing themselves and practicing their walks to school."

"And that's when I saw them," Abby added.

"But you didn't see where they ended up, did you?" Cam asked.

"Nope."

"But we have evidence of where they ended up," Cam went on. "Do you still have the paper?"

"I do," Abby said, pulling out the stained paper.

"We already figured out that the stain is chocolate milk," Cam said. "And that the letters and numbers mean 128 IN 3, or one hundred twenty-eight divided by three."

"Which can't be done," Gabe said. "At least not into equal whole numbers. But what did they have one hundred twenty-eight of?"

"Ounces," Cam said. "There are one hundred twenty-eight ounces in a gallon."

Gabe turned to Abby for confirmation, and Abby nodded.

"If you remember at lunch today, the triplets had a gallon of chocolate milk that they were splitting up between the three of them," Cam went on. "I think they were doing the same thing yesterday. Like it was their celebratory drink. Only they were pouring it in Mrs. E.'s room, which is where they ended up."

"Because it was the final stop on their practice walks to school," Gabe said, his face lighting up in recognition.

"Exactly," Cam said. "They were trying to figure out how much chocolate milk each of them would get, but then they spilled it on the paper."

"And since the paper was wet, they couldn't finish the equation," Gabe added.

"You betcha," Cam said. "And when they cleaned it up, they forgot to clean up the paper, probably because it was under a desk or something, and that's how it got stuck to Gabe's foot this morning."

"What about the iPad?" Abby said.

"They snatched it on their way out," Cam said with a shrug. "Simple."

"It's an interesting theory," Gabe said. "But there are a few flaws."

Cam put his hand on his chest. "It seems pretty flawless to me."

"What about the locked door?" Gabe said. "How did they open the locked door?"

Cam thought for a few seconds and then said, "With lock picks? Or stolen keys? Or—"

"They're kids," Gabe said. "Not bank robbers. But they are smart. I'll give them that. Because I'm pretty sure they did come in through this window."

"Uh-uh," Cam said. "Remember there are two problems with that. We didn't see any fingerprints. Plus, Abby would've spotted the triplets near the window yesterday. But she saw them going toward the front entrance."

"We didn't see any fingerprints because they were using gloves or something else covering their hands," Gabe said. "And Abby didn't see them near the window because they opened it after she went home. Remember how they told us that they practiced the walk to school three times? They said they timed one another individually, while the other two cheered their brother on."

"They did say that, didn't they?" Abby remarked.

"Maybe you were watching their first attempt," Gabe said. "And maybe later, after the third attempt, they opened the window when no one was watching."

"What about footprints?" Cam asked. "There were no footprints in the mud by the window. Are you saying they did it before it started raining?"

"Maybe," Gabe said. "Or maybe they placed something next to the window that they could climb on. You know, so they didn't leave footprints? It would have to be something that left three rectangular prints in the mud instead."

"What sort of something?" Abby asked.

Gabe smiled a smug smile and then paced with confidence across the schoolyard toward the toolshed. The other two had no choice but to follow.

When he got there, Cam heard strange sounds coming from inside the shed, like chirps and growls and whistles. But soon his attention shifted to the real reason they were there. Gabe was standing next to . . .

"A wheelbarrow?" Cam asked.

It was indeed a wheelbarrow. Gabe smiled another smug smile, then turned and pushed the wheelbarrow back toward the window. Again,

Cam and Abby followed, and when they were all near the mud, Gabe guided the wheelbarrow's rubber wheel into one of the three indentations.

It fit perfectly. When he lowered the rest of the wheelbarrow down, the two metal supports fit into the other indentations. "Like a key in a lock," he said with a proud smile.

"So, you're saying the Pendertons placed the wheelbarrow here, got inside it, opened the window using something over their hands, then climbed into Mrs. E.'s room and stole the iPad?" Abby asked.

Gabe nodded. "But they also did what Cam said. They spilled their gallon of chocolate milk in the room and cleaned it up but left the paper behind."

"See," Cam said proudly. "I'm right."

"We both are," Gabe said.

"You're both right," Abby said. "But I think you're also both wrong."

"What?" the two boys said at the same time.

"I have another theory," Abby said. "But I think we need to talk to the custodian,

Mrs. Vernon, first. As well as Mrs. E. Not to mention the triplets."

"You mean the *treacherous* triplets," Gabe said. "Clearly they've been pretending to be nicer, and more clueless, than they really are."

"And in case you forgot, there's still the possibility that they tried to injure me on the playground," Cam said.

"I didn't forget," Abby said. "But I think there's more to it. Come with me."

Chapter 10

THE CASE OF THE MISSING IPAD

The crowd outside of Arithmos Elementary was growing bigger. It seemed like every student, teacher, and their families were there for the bonfire. It was no surprise. The weather was warm and pleasant, with clear skies and very little wind.

As the Prime Detectives searched the crowd, people kept on stopping them and asking them questions.

"I lost my violin. Can you do some equations that will help me find it?" Sanjeev asked Gabe.

"If those triplets try to give us cookies again, would you mind being our poison taster?" Luciana asked Cam.

"Are there computer chips in your brain,

and is that why you're so good at calculations?" Maisie asked Abby.

The Prime Detectives were polite, but they couldn't spend time fielding all these questions. They needed to—

"There!" Cam shouted, pointing through the crowd at the custodian, Mrs. Vernon. She wasn't dressed in her standard khaki uniform, so it wasn't immediately obvious that it was her. But she was Cam's neighbor, and he recognized her husband before he recognized her. They were holding hands and eating ice cream.

"Mrs. Vernon! Mrs. Vernon!" Abby called out as she rushed to her.

It took Mrs. Vernon a few moments to figure out who was saying her name, but when she did, a large smile sprouted on her face. She had helped the Prime Detectives with a few mysteries in the past. But she wasn't always the best at remembering names.

"Well, if it isn't the girl they call the Slide Rule," she said.

"The what?" Cam asked.

"Another computational device," Gabe told him. "Invented in the 1600s. Well before the calculator but long after the abacus."

"The Abacus!" Mrs. Vernon said while slapping a hand on her forehead. "My mistake. You're Abby the Abacus. And with your little friends here, you're the Ace Investigators, right?"

"Exactly," Abby said, because she didn't want to embarrass Mrs. Vernon again by correcting her. "And we need your help with a solution."

"She solves everything for me," Mr. Vernon said with a smile. "I'm sure she can do the same for you."

"I'll try, at least," Mrs. Vernon said.

"We just need to know about yesterday," Gabe said. "Abby saw you outside yesterday afternoon. What were you doing?"

One thing Gabe had learned while solving mysteries was that direct questions didn't always get you the answers you needed. It was always better to have people simply tell their stories without leading them one way or another.

Because then they'd reveal more details. And since the witnesses and suspects didn't usually know what the Prime Detectives already knew, Gabe could sometimes catch them in a lie.

When Mrs. Vernon spoke, it certainly didn't seem like she was lying. She was friendly and helpful, telling them, "I spent yesterday afternoon clearing sticks from the schoolyard so we could use them as kindling for the bonfire this evening. The wheelbarrow made quick work of it. Not much to say other than that."

"Is that all you did?" Gabe asked.

"Pests are a constant problem around here, so I set a few traps to catch some around the school," Mrs. Vernon said. "Oh, and I also cleaned Mrs. E.'s room."

"Really?" Gabe said. "Tell us about cleaning Mrs. E.'s room."

"I was almost done collecting sticks when it started to rain, so I left my wheelbarrow next to that window over there," Mrs. Vernon said, pointing to the window to Mrs. E.'s room. "I looked in, and I saw that there was some liquid on the floor. I went inside to investigate. The liquid was spilling into the hall when I got there, so I unlocked the door and found a big puddle of chocolate milk. Half of it was in the room, and half was in the hall."

Gabe nodded at Cam in recognition that he was right.

"I mopped up the chocolate milk," Mrs. Vernon said. "Then I went down to my office to get ready for today. When I noticed that it had stopped raining, I went back to Mrs. E.'s room and I opened the window so that the floors would dry and so that it wouldn't smell like cleaning chemicals in there. Then I went home."

This was huge! Mrs. Vernon was in Mrs. E.'s room. She had admitted to it. Which rocketed her to the top of the suspect list. But the Prime Detectives weren't about to accuse her of anything. Not yet at least. Again, it was better to ask general questions.

"Did you notice anything on Mrs. E.'s desk?" Gabe asked.

Mrs. Vernon shrugged. "Normal stuff on the desk, I guess. Nothing strange in the room that I remember. Besides the chocolate milk."

Gabe knew that if she had stolen the iPad, she certainly wouldn't have admitted it. But he also knew that guilty people often add details to their stories to prove their "innocence."

If Mrs. Vernon was guilty, she might've lied and mentioned that the iPad was there when she left. But she didn't seem to notice it either way. Which was interesting, even if it didn't rule her out as a suspect.

"I think that's all we need to know," Abby said cheerfully. "Thanks, Mrs. Vernon."

"Anytime, Ace Investigators," she said with a smile. Then Mrs. Vernon and her husband walked off hand in hand.

"That wasn't all we needed to know," Gabe said under his breath as he smiled and waved at the departing Vernons. "She's still a suspect."

"I don't think so," Abby said. "Besides, I spotted some other people we need to talk to."

All three of them were walking toward the mound of sticks and brush that would soon become the bonfire. It was Jason, Mason, and Grayson. The Penderton triplets were here!

Q

"Gotcha," Cam said as he, Gabe, and Abby snuck up behind Jason, Mason, and Grayson.

The triplets all jumped in surprise and nearly tripped over one another as they turned around. When they regained their composure, Jason put a hand over his heart and said, "Oh, it's you. We're so glad to see you."

"You are?" Gabe asked, because he figured the three of them would be wary of the Prime Detectives by now.

"For sure," said Mason. "You really helped us today."

"And we have something we want to get off our chests," Grayson said.

Cam and Gabe both gave each other the same look: *Is this really happening?*

At the same time, the triplets all said, "Yesterday afternoon we—"

But Gabe cut them off. "Stole Mrs. E.'s iPad. We know."

"Did you pick the lock?" Cam asked.

"Or did you come back to school at night and climb onto the wheelbarrow and in through the open window?" Gabe asked.

"No," Jason said, aghast.

"Gross," Mason said, even more aghast.

"That's ridiculous," Grayson said, the most aghast.

"But, but, but you told us you wanted to get something off your chest," Cam said.

"Not about stealing anything," Grayson said.

"We only wanted to confess about spilling some chocolate milk," Jason said.

"Well, we already know you did that," Gabe said with a huff.

Mason threw up his hands. "Of course you do! You know everything."

"Not everything," Abby said. "Tell us what exactly happened with the chocolate milk."

"We know what happened," Gabe said. "They spilled it in Mrs. E.'s room."

"That's not exactly right," Mason said.

"We spilled it in the hall *outside of* Mrs. E.'s room," Jason said.

"And then we tried to clean it up with the only thing we had," Grayson said.

"This piece of paper?" Abby asked, and she pulled out the stained page with 128 IN 3 on it.

"Wow! Yes, that's the one!" Jason said. "It didn't work very well."

"It just pushed the milk under the door and into Mrs. E.'s room," Grayson added.

"And then the paper got stuck to the bottom of the door when we tried to use it to stop the flow," Mason said.

It took a couple of moments, but then something dawned on Gabe, and he put a finger up in recognition. "Which would explain why it got stuck to my foot when I left the room this morning."

Abby and Cam nodded in agreement.

"And that's another reason why we wanted to be at school early," Jason said. "We wanted to clean up our mess. But we all remember how that worked out."

"So, you never went into the room and stole the iPad?" Cam asked.

"Of course not," Mason said.

"We're clumsy," Jason said.

"But we're not thieves," Grayson said.

"And neither is Mrs. Vernon," Abby said. "She has the opportunity to steal things every day, so why would she steal something now, especially since she admitted she was in the room where it was stolen from?"

"Good point," Gabe admitted.

"Do we have another suspect?" Cam asked.

Abby looked up to the sky. The sun was getting low, and birds were silhouetted against the clouds in the purple glow of dusk.

"At least three," Abby said. "Let's go find Mrs. E."

It took a while.

The Penderton triplets helped the Prime Detectives look for Mrs. E., but even with six of them searching, it was difficult to spot anyone in the thick crowd of students, teachers, and parents. It also didn't help that they were trying to spot Mrs. E.'s equation dress, without knowing she had gone home and changed out of it.

Their teacher was now wearing a black dress decorated with red and orange flames. Which meant she would be more or less camouflaged once the bonfire started. Thankfully, it hadn't, so Abby was able to spot her.

"There," she said, pointing through the crowd to their teacher and a tall handsome man holding her hand.

"Who's that with Mrs. E.?" Cam asked.

"Mr. E?" Gabe said.

"It may be a mystery to you," Cam replied, "but I bet someone knows the guy's name."

Before Gabe could explain to Cam what he'd meant, the guy was gone, and Mrs. E. was standing right next to the kids as if she had teleported there.

"Hey, gang," she said.

"Mrs. E.!" Abby cried. "We're so glad to see you."

"And I'm so glad to see all of you together," Mrs. E. said. "It's a long year, and I want all my students to get along with and trust each other."

The triplets nodded, then eventually Cam and Gabe nodded, too. But Abby spoke. "We know the Pendertons made some mistakes, but we all make mistakes."

"And we know they didn't steal your iPad," Gabe said, which made the Pendertons smile.

"But we're still trying to figure out who did," Cam added. "Abby says she has three other suspects."

"Oh, no, no, no," Mrs. E. said. "I don't want anyone pointing any more fingers. We saw how that worked out earlier."

"I think these three suspects can deal with the accusations," Abby said. "In fact, I think they'll fly right past them."

"Okay," Mrs. E. said. "I'm intrigued."

"I'll explain," Abby said. "This morning when we came into class, there was a black-feathered bird on your desk."

"You called it a birdbrain," Cam said. "Which was pretty funny."

"I remember," Mrs. E. said with a smile. "I hope I didn't hurt its feelings."

"Later in the day, we met Mr. Mortimer Sunshine, and we learned about how big some birds used to be," Abby said.

"Bigger than me!" Cam said.

"And probably big enough to pick you up," Abby said.

"I think I see where you're going with this," Mrs. E. said.

"I bet you do," Abby said. "Because you're a bird expert, and I'm just an amateur. But one thing I've always heard is that birds like shiny objects. That they often steal shiny objects to put in their nests."

"That is a common belief," Mrs. E. said.

"And your iPad has a shiny rhinestone cover, right?" Abby asked.

"It does," Mrs. E. said.

"Wait," Gabe said. "Are you saying that the little bird from this morning stole the iPad?"

"No, that was a grackle," Abby said. "Too small. And besides, the iPad was already gone by then."

"You better not be accusing Mr. Mortimer Sunshine," Cam said with a gasp. "Anyone but that sweet little budgie!"

Abby smiled. "Not him, either."

"Then who?" the triplets asked.

"Well," Abby said. "I borrowed a book about birds from the library, and it had a lot of helpful information to narrow down some suspects. Let's look at some numbers, why don't we."

Abby wrote the following things with a pencil on a white popcorn bag.

ITEM	WEIGHT
IPAD	17 OUNCES
RHINESTONE CASE	23 OUNCES
RAVEN	1¼ KILOGRAMS CARRYING STRENGTH: EQUAL TO WEIGHT
BALD EAGLE	5¼ KILOGRAMS CARRYING STRENGTH: 1/3 OF WEIGHT
RED-TAILED HAWK	800 GRAMS CARRYING STRENGTH: 150% OF WEIGHT

CONVERSION CHART		
16 OUNCES	=	1 POUND
454 GRAMS	=	1 POUND
1,000 GRAMS	=	1 KILOGRAM

"What are we supposed to do with all of that?" Jason Penderton asked.

"The raven, the bald eagle, and the red-tailed hawk are all large birds that I have observed near the school," Abby explained. "I checked the library's bird book to see how big they were and how much weight they could carry. I also investigated the weight of the iPad and its case. Some of the information was written in grams and kilograms, which is the metric system. And other information was in pounds and ounces, which is the imperial system. I provided the conversions so we can switch between the two."

"You mean someone is supposed to do these calculations?" Mason asked.

"I've already done them," Abby said.

"Obviously," Cam said.

"But I wanted you to all understand how to figure out which of these birds, if any, could've carried the iPad out the open window," Abby said.

"You seriously believe that's what happened?" Gabe asked.

Abby nodded confidently.

"Fine," Gabe said. "I'll do the calculations."

But Mrs. E. butted in. "Hold on a sec. I think the triplets can do the calculations."

The Pendertons looked terrified as all three of them said, "I don't think so."

"All you need is a little confidence," Mrs. E. said with a wink. "Plus, I think you've learned a lot today and can figure it out."

"And if you need any help, we're right here," Abby said.

Chapter 11

BIRDBRAINS

The Penderton triplets put on their thinking caps. Literally. They each had identical knit caps that they pulled out of their pockets and pulled over their heads. All three sat in a circle and worked on equations as the Prime Detectives and Mrs. E. looked on.

"Okay, first thing we have to do is figure out how much the bird was carrying, right?" Jason said.

"Right," Mason said. "It's the weight of the iPad plus the weight of the rhinestone case."

"Seventeen ounces plus twenty-three ounces," Grayson said.

"Easy," Jason said. "Forty ounces."

EVIDENCE

17 + 23 = 40 40 OUNCES
OUNCES (IPAD) OUNCES (CASE) OUNCES TOTAL

"But how many pounds is that?" Grayson asked.

"There are sixteen ounces in a pound," Mason said. "And two sixteens are thirty-two."

$$16 \times 2 = 32 \quad \longrightarrow \quad 32 = 2$$
OUNCES OUNCES   OUNCES POUNDS

"That means it's two pounds with eight ounces left over," Grayson said. "Because forty minus thirty-two equals eight."

$$40 - 32 = 8 \quad \longrightarrow \quad 8 \text{ OUNCES}$$
OUNCES OUNCES   were left over

"That's right," Abby confirmed.

Jason had written it all down on a popcorn bag.

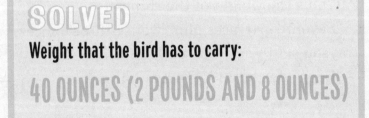

SOLVED

Weight that the bird has to carry:

40 OUNCES (2 POUNDS AND 8 OUNCES)

"Okay, now we have to see which bird could carry that much," Jason said.

"The Raven weighs one and one quarter kilograms," Mason said. "How many grams are in a quarter kilogram?"

Grayson pointed to the spot where Abby wrote the conversions and said, "Abby showed us that there are one thousand grams in a kilogram. So, to figure out how many grams are in a quarter of a kilogram, we divide one thousand by four."

"Which is two hundred fifty," Jason said.

1 KILOGRAM = 1,000 GRAMS
1,000 ÷ 4 = 250 GRAMS

THERE ARE 250 GRAMS IN ¼ KILOGRAM

"But since the raven weighs one and one quarter kilograms, we need to add that two hundred fifty to one thousand," Grayson said. "And we get one thousand two hundred fifty grams."

"Remember, Abby wrote that a raven could carry its own weight," Mason said. "Which means it can carry . . ."

Jason jotted down:

250 + 1,000 = 1,250
GRAMS   GRAMS   GRAMS

RAVEN
CAN CARRY 1,250 GRAMS

"But we need to convert that to ounces or pounds to see if a raven could carry the iPad and case, right?" Grayson asked.

"Let's figure out the others first," Jason said. "Then we'll convert at the end."

"That does sound more exciting," Cam said, because he appreciated a bit of suspense.

"The bald eagle weighs five and one quarter kilograms. Five kilograms is five thousand grams, and we just learned a quarter kilogram is two hundred fifty grams, right?" Mason asked.

"Right," Abby said.

"Add them up and you get five thousand two hundred fifty grams," Grayson said.

5,000 + 250 = 5,250

"But it can only carry one third of its weight," Jason said. "Meaning we have to divide five thousand two hundred fifty by three. Does that work?"

"Remember the trick," Grayson said.

Jason wrote it all out:

$$5 + 2 + 5 + 0 = 12 \implies 1 + 2 = 3$$

"It can be divided by three!" the triplets shouted.

"But how will you figure out what that equals?" Mrs. E. asked.

"I can't do it in my head easily," Jason said. "But I can round up to the nearest number where I can. I know that six thousand divided by three is two thousand, because six divided by two is three. And then you just add three zeroes because we're talking about thousands."

$$6,000 \div 3 = 2,000$$

"And *I* know that six thousand minus five thousand two hundred fifty is seven hundred fifty," Mason said. "Because it's just like six hundred minus five hundred twenty-five, which is seventy-five, but then you add a zero on the end."

$$6,000 - 5,250 = 750$$

"Seven hundred fifty needs to be divided by three," Grayson said. "Which is the same as seventy-five divided by three, with an extra zero added at the end. In other words, two hundred fifty."

$$750 \div 3 = 250$$

"Then we subtract that two hundred fifty from two thousand," Grayson said. "Which is just like two hundred minus twenty-five, with a zero added at the end."

"Or one thousand seven hundred fifty grams," Jason said.

$$2,000 - 250 = 1,750$$

"What does that mean?" Mrs. E. asked.

Jason must have forgotten what they were originally calculating at first, but then it dawned on him, and he jotted something else on the popcorn bag. He held it up for all to see.

$$5{,}250 \div 3 = 1{,}750$$

GRAMS   GRAMS

BALD EAGLE
CAN CARRY 1,750 GRAMS

"That leaves the red-tailed hawk," Mason said.

"This one is easy," Grayson said. "Because we already know it weighs eight hundred grams. But what does 150 percent of its weight mean?"

"It means one and a half times its weight," Jason said.

"You were paying attention when Luciana and I were talking about percentages earlier, weren't you?" Gabe said.

Jason nodded proudly.

"So, we need eight hundred plus half of eight hundred." Mason said. "Half of eight hundred is easy. Because it's like half of eight, with two zeros added. Which is four hundred. Add them together and we get . . ."

"One thousand two hundred grams," the triplets said at the same time.

"Exactly right," Abby told them.

And Jason wrote down:

$$800 \div 2 = 400$$

$$\underset{\text{GRAMS}}{800} + \underset{\text{GRAMS}}{400} = \underset{\text{GRAMS}}{1,200} \rightarrow \text{RED-TAILED HAWK}$$
CAN CARRY 1,200 GRAMS

"Now all we have to do is convert all the grams to ounces and pounds," Grayson said. "Then we'll be able to figure out if each bird could've carried the iPad."

"But we'd have to convert three times," Jason told him.

"That's right," Mason said. "If we convert the ounces to grams, we only have to do it once."

"I see," Grayson said. "And Abby told us there are four hundred fifty-four grams in a pound. So, we just have to multiply four hundred fifty-four by two pounds and eight ounces, which is the weight of the iPad and its case."

"Let's start by multiplying by the two pounds and deal with the eight ounces later," Jason said. "Two times four hundred fifty-four is easy. "First we take four hundred fifty and multiply it by two, which is the same as forty-five times two, with an extra zero at the end."

$$450 \times 2 = 900$$

Mason jumped in for the next step of the equation. "Then we take the four we have left over and multiply it by two to get eight."

$$4 \times 2 = 8$$

Grayson finished things off by saying, "Add it all together, and we get nine hundred eight."

$$900 + 8 = 908$$
GRAMS GRAMS GRAMS → 908 GRAMS
in 2 pounds

"But we still have to convert those eight ounces to grams?" Mason said.

"It's not that hard," Grayson said. "Because eight ounces is exactly half of sixteen ounces, and sixteen ounces is a pound."

$$16 \div 2 = 8$$
OUNCES   OUNCES

➡

8 OUNCES
is ½ a pound

"Which means eight ounces is half a pound," Jason said excitedly. "But we need to know what half of four hundred fifty-four is, because there are four hundred fifty-four grams in a pound."

The triplets started talking and calculating and jotting down numbers so fast that it was impossible to tell who was saying and doing what.

"I can round up, and I know that half of four hundred sixty is two hundred thirty, because half of forty-six is twenty-three, then we add a zero on the end."

$$460 \div 2 = 230$$

"And four hundred sixty minus four hundred fifty-four is six."

$$460 - 454 = 6$$

"And half of six is three."

$$6 \div 2 = 3$$

"And two hundred thirty minus three is two hundred twenty-seven."

$$230 - 3 = 227$$

"That's how many grams there are in half a pound, but we have to add that number to the nine hundred eight grams that are in two pounds, and we get . . ."

"One thousand one hundred thirty-five ounces!" they all shouted at the same time, and they held up their popcorn bag, which showed the work they had done.

$$227 + 908 = (200 + 900) + (27 + 8)$$
$$200 + 900 = 1,100 \text{ and } 27 + 8 = 35$$
$$\text{So, } 1,100 + 35 = 1,135$$
$$\text{And therefore } 227 + 908 = 1,135$$

"That's right!" Abby said.

"Now what does all that mean?" Mrs. E. asked them.

Jason frantically jotted down what they figured out through the conversions, then he held it up for everyone to see.

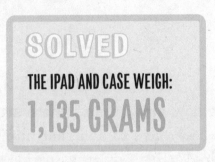

SOLVED

THE IPAD AND CASE WEIGH:

1,135 GRAMS

"See what you can accomplish when you work together," Mrs. E. said.

The triplets all smiled proudly. Until they didn't. Because they noticed something.

"Wait," Jason said. "If the iPad weighs that much . . ."

"And each bird can carry more than that . . ." Mason said.

"Then all three birds are still suspects, aren't they?" Grayson asked.

Abby sighed. "Yeah, that's the conclusion I reached, too. I was hoping someone else would find something that ruled them out. Can anybody rule any of the birds out?"

Abby was greeted with shrugs from Cam and Gabe and Grayson and Mason and Jason. The excitement was gone. They had officially hit a wall in the investigation. Until . . .

Mrs. E. put a hand on Abby's shoulder. "Maybe I can rule them *all* out," she said. "Because you made one small mistake."

Cam and Gabe gasped. This was unheard of! Unprecedented! Unbelievable!

"In my calculations?" Abby the Abacus said.

"No," Mrs. E. said. "In your assumptions. See, there's a common myth that birds like shiny things and steal them for their nests. But that's never been proven true. In fact, shiny things often scare birds away. That's why I hang aluminum pie plates over my berry bushes."

"So, if it wasn't the triplets, and it wasn't Mrs. Vernon, and it wasn't the birds, then who the heck was it?" Cam asked.

"I think someone may have already caught the perpetrator," Mrs. E. said. "And I think the perpetrator is still here."

Mrs. E. led the six kids through the schoolyard until they found Mrs. Vernon again. She and her husband were heading toward the bonfire, which was going to be lit in a few minutes.

"Hey, gang," Mrs. Vernon said when she saw them. "The firefighters are in position. Wanna go see them light it up?"

"In a moment," Mrs. E. said. "First, I was wondering if you could show our friends the troublemaker you caught last night. Is our rascally friend still here?"

"Our rascally friend *is* still here," Mrs. Vernon said. "At least for a few more minutes. In the toolshed. I don't see a problem with introducing the kids. But everyone needs to stand back."

Was Mrs. Vernon keeping a person in the toolshed? That seemed . . . problematic. But they needed to solve this mystery, so the kids followed and didn't say a word.

"Everyone, stay outside," Mrs. Vernon said as she unlocked and opened the door to the shed. "Our friend might not be happy to see visitors."

The shed was well organized, with tools either hung up on hooks or resting against the walls. In the middle, there was something with a blanket over the top of it.

"Is that what we saw you wheeling near the school this morning?" Abby asked. The morning seemed like ages ago, so Abby wasn't surprised that she didn't remember the moment until now.

"Something was making a weird sound under the blanket," Gabe added.

And Cam cringed as he asked, "Was it a kid?"

This made Mrs. Vernon laugh. "It's a young one for sure," she said as she pulled the blanket up to reveal a small cage underneath. In that cage, there was a raccoon. Even though the raccoon bared its teeth and snarled, it was still pretty cute.

"Ooh," the Penderton triplets cooed when they saw it.

"You were carrying that cage yesterday," Abby said as she naturally dipped back into her Memory Palace to recall what she had seen in the schoolyard. "When you were collecting sticks. I thought it was a dog crate."

"This little raccoon kept sneaking into the school and stealing things," Mrs. Vernon said. "So, to catch it, I placed this trap near its den in that hollowed-out log over there."

Mrs. Vernon pointed to a spot in the distance where the schoolyard was bordered by the forest.

"Raccoon traps use shiny objects to attract raccoons," Mrs. E. told the kids.

"That's right," Mrs. Vernon said. "And this morning, after I dumped the sticks from the wheelbarrow, I noticed that the trap had worked. So, I brought the raccoon to the shed until it could be collected by a professional."

"Do you think this raccoon stole the iPad?" Gabe said.

"I'm almost sure of it," Mrs. E. said.

"Why? Did you find the iPad in its den?" Cam asked Mrs. Vernon with hope in his voice. "Or anywhere near its den?"

"I looked in the den and there were some scraps of foil and other small objects, but nothing as fancy as that," Mrs. E. said.

"Then how do you know the raccoon stole it?" Gabe asked Mrs. E.

Mrs. E. was about to speak when Abby jumped in.

"I think I've got it all figured out," Abby said. "Do you mind if I break it down for everyone?"

"Please do," Mrs. E. said.

"Okay," Abby said. "This is what happened yesterday. Mrs. Vernon set some traps to catch some pests, including the trap for this raccoon. She also collected some sticks for the bonfire in her wheelbarrow. When it started raining, she left the wheelbarrow full of sticks by the window to Mrs. E.'s room. Then she went inside to clean up the chocolate milk. When it stopped raining, she opened the window to Mrs. E.'s room and went home. Sometime in the night, the raccoon climbed onto the wheelbarrow and in through the window. It was attracted to the shiny rhinestones on the iPad case, so it stole it. When the raccoon was returning to its den, it got caught in the trap. In the morning, Mrs. Vernon dumped the sticks out of the wheelbarrow and onto the bonfire. Then she found the raccoon in the cage, covered the cage with a blanket, and wheeled it out to the shed. Does that sound right?"

"On the money," Mrs. Vernon said. "I feel bad that I left that window open. But we all make mistakes, right?"

The Pendertons nodded in agreement.

"But where did the iPad go?" Gabe said.

"Yeah," Cam added. "If it wasn't in or near the den, where did the raccoon put it?"

One of the Pendertons decided to field this question. "What if the raccoon dropped it in the wheelbarrow?" Grayson said.

And his brothers backed him up.

"Yeah," Mason said. "When we did all those calculations about whether a bird could carry an iPad, we figured out that it was possible. But we never figured out how far they could carry it. Or if they could even carry something shaped like an iPad."

"The same is probably true of the raccoon," Jason said. "Maybe it could've dragged the iPad across Mrs. E.'s desk, over to the counter, out the window, and into the wheelbarrow. But could it carry it all the way back to its den?"

"Probably not," Cam said.

"Yeah, that's a good point," Gabe said. "Maybe there's a calculation we could use to figure out how far a raccoon could carry—"

"I don't think we need to do that," Abby said, "because I don't think there's time for math right now. If the Pendertons are right, and I think they might be, the raccoon dropped the iPad in the wheelbarrow full of sticks, and the wheelbarrow full of sticks was dumped over there."

Abby pointed to the pile of wood where the bonfire was supposed to be. And all the kids gasped because that wood was doing what it was put there to do.

It was burning.

Chapter 12

THREE PLUS
THREE IS SIX

The bonfire raged, its flames twisting and slapping against the evening sky.

"Oh no," Gabe said. "The iPad is in there."

"There's no saving it now," Abby said.

"We did all that math for nothing!" Cam cried.

It was too late, and too dangerous, to pull anything from the bonfire. Even if they wanted to try, the firefighters surrounding it certainly wouldn't let them. They were standing guard, making sure everyone was a safe distance away.

All the kids could do now was stare at the flames, lamenting a lost cause. "Do you think we were right, though?" Jason asked.

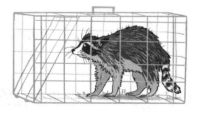

"I not only think it," Mrs. E. said. "I know it."

"And how do you know it?" Mason said.

"Yeah," Grayson said. "The iPad is probably melted by now. There won't be any evidence."

"Maybe I should tell you about my day," Mrs. E. said. "That should clear things up."

"It won't get your iPad out of the fire, though," Gabe said.

"I still think you'll want to hear this," Mrs. E. said. Then she sat down in the grass and motioned for everyone else to sit, which they did. "I arrived this morning before the buses, and I unlocked my classroom and went to the teacher's lounge to say hello to friends and colleagues. When I got back to my room, I met Gabe, Abby, and Cam. And that was when I first noticed the iPad was missing."

"And you picked up your abacus," Abby reminded her.

"That's right," Mrs. E. said. "And I used that abacus for the rest of the day. I also searched for my iPad and asked people if they had seen it. I didn't think a student or anyone who worked at the school would have stolen it. So, when Mrs. Vernon stopped by the classroom after recess and she told me she had caught the raccoon, I started to think that maybe the raccoon was a suspect.

After all, the window to my room was open throughout the night. And raccoons love shiny things. Once classes were over, I went outside to investigate. I noticed some strange prints on the ground next to my window."

"The wheelbarrow," Gabe said.

"I wasn't as clever as you," Mrs. E. said. "I didn't figure that part out. But as I was looking for more clues in the schoolyard, a helpful firefighter told me they found something in the wood for the bonfire."

That's when Mrs. E. held up the iPad. *The* iPad. Still in its rhinestone case. No longer missing and not charred or melted at all.

"It's okay?" Abby asked.

Mrs. E. nodded and said, "I was lucky. But the three of you . . ." She paused and then turned to the Penderton triplets. "I'm sorry, I mean the *six* of you . . . you figured everything out. Without any luck. You used math, logic, and teamwork. And you solved the case. I'm proud of each of you."

It felt especially good to hear these words. Abby, Cam, and Gabe knew how smart and kind and special Mrs. E. was, so hearing that she was proud of them was the only reward they needed for solving the mystery. It appeared that the

Pendertons were feeling the same thing. They were absolutely beaming.

Gabe was still curious about something, though. "There is one thing that continues to bother me," he said. "After Cam got knocked over by the balls, the triplets disappeared. Where did they go?"

"Do you mind if I tell him?" Mrs. E. asked, and the triplets nodded their approval. "The Pendertons came to find me to apologize. For being late, for the cookies—"

"And for spilling the chocolate milk the day before," Jason said.

Mrs. E. nodded. "I forgave them, of course. These were all mistakes. We all make mistakes. Plus, they wanted to make amends."

"We also asked her if it was okay to make our triple chocolate chip cookies again and bring them to the bonfire to share," Jason said.

"But don't worry," Mason said. "We got the recipe right this time."

"And we made sure to taste-test them first," Grayson said. "They're delicious."

The three boys each had backpacks with them. And they each reached inside and pulled out something. Jason pulled out a bag of cookies.

Mason pulled out a gallon of chocolate milk. And Grayson pulled out plastic cups and paper napkins.

Mrs. E. turned to Cam. "Would our favorite supertaster like to be the first one to try one?"

Jason opened the bag and presented a cookie while Mason and Grayson poured some chocolate milk. To be honest, Cam was a little scared. But all the evidence pointed to the fact that triplets were trustworthy and that they learned from their mistakes.

That's why Cam took the cookie, sniffed the cookie, bit the cookie, chewed the cookie, and swallowed the cookie, which he followed up with a big gulp of chocolate milk.

"So . . . ?" Gabe asked.

Cam took a deep breath. Then he smiled. "You three could teach me a thing or two. These cookies are AMAZING!"

The rest of the evening was full of fun, food, and friends. The Pendertons shared the cookies with their other classmates, and they all gathered around the bonfire and sang the school song.

The triplets learned the lyrics quickly and

joined in a rousing rendition. As first days go, it was among the most memorable at Arithmos Elementary. But the Prime Detectives knew there were still a lot of days ahead of them, and a lot of memories to make and mysteries to solve.

Before the evening was over, a man named Ricky stopped by the shed to pick up the raccoon, and the gang went to see the cute little thief off.

"What will happen to it?" Abby asked.

"Well, this little rascal is lucky," Ricky said. "Most raccoons can't be relocated. It's not safe for them or people. But I'm a conservationist who specializes in these cases. It's a good thing Mrs. Vernon called me. I'll have a veterinarian test the raccoon for rabies and other diseases, and then we'll bring it to a special sanctuary where he can be with some new friends."

"Just make sure you don't leave any iPads around," Cam said.

This puzzled Ricky, until Gabe explained what happened.

"Don't worry," Ricky said with a laugh. "We'll limit its screen time."

And then he was off, carrying the cage and the raccoon back to his van.

The Prime Detectives and the Penderton triplets made one more lap around the schoolyard, saying *See you tomorrow* to all their friends and teachers, and joking with each other about all the things that happened. When it was time to say goodbye, the Prime Detectives did something that was always good to do. They apologized.

"I'm sorry your first day was so lousy," Cam said.

"And I'm sorry we contributed to that," Abby added.

"And I'm sorry we had to teach you all that math," Gabe said.

The triplets laughed it off.

"No apologies necessary," Mason said.

"Yeah," Jason said. "We couldn't have asked for a more exciting first day."

"And we helped solve a mystery," Grayson said.

"That's the truth," Cam said. "We can't always solve these mysteries alone."

"So, we might ask for your help again in the future," Abby said.

"Though maybe we'll double-check your math," Gabe said.

The triplets laughed this off, too. They were good kids, the furthest thing from treacherous, and it was clear that they would thrive at Arithmos Elementary.

A few minutes later, Abby, Cam, and Gabe said their final goodbyes, and they joined back up with their parents, piled into the backs of their respective cars, and headed home.

The Penderton triplets didn't need a car, of course. They lived nearby, so they decided to walk home. Or, to be more accurate, they decided to run. They made it back in record time. And they knew that when school started the next day, they'd be the first three there.

ACKNOWLEDGMENTS

Beka Wallin + Emily Stone + Mia Moran + Michael Bourret + Mindy Fichter + Jason Wang + Christina Quintero + Justin Krasner + Caitlyn Hunter + Nathalie LeDu = THIS BOOK

 It could not exist without them. For that, they deserve innumerable thanks.

AARON STARMER is the author of more than a dozen novels for young readers. Unlike many authors, he really enjoys math. This is his first mystery. He lives in Vermont with his wife and two daughters.

MARTA KISSI is a Bath-based illustrator, originally from Warsaw. She studied illustration and animation at Kingston University and visual communication at the Royal College of Art. Her favorite part of being an illustrator is bringing stories to life by designing charming characters and the wonderful worlds they live in. She shares her artist studio with her husband, James, and their pet plant, Trevor.

MORE MYSTERIES TO UNRAVEL!

Join the Prime Detectives in

Math Mysteries

THE FALL FESTIVAL FIASCO

Available soon wherever books are sold.